TORUSSIA
WITHLOVE

ISBN: 978-1-968970-41-3 Paperback
ISBN: 978-1-968970-42-0 Ebook

Rev. date: 08/26/2025

TORUSSIA WITHLOVE

H.D. Duman

CONTENTS

ACKNOWLEDGEMENT

I am indebted to Leavitt Peak Press for accepting my manuscript and publishing To Russia With Love. A special thanks as well as well to my Beta readers for putting up with me. I deliberately blurred the lines, in some cases, between fact and fiction in order to give the story more impact and mystery. Any omissions and/errors are, of course, all mine. The characters are entirely fictitious and any resemblance to persons living or dead is purely coincidental.

Likewise, I would like to thank operations manager Mia Baker for her input and efforts to this project.

Finally, what can I say about my sr. publicist, Lucy Lane? She has been supporting my efforts the whole time.

PROLOGUE

Iran -2016

A plane load of cash arrived in Iran to appease the Ayatollah Ali Khamanel to release 4 US citizens. The cash had been in US greenbacks, Euros, Swiss Francs, and other currencies. The Boeing carrying the 400 million had been a partial payment of $1.7 billion. Iran had initially requested $10 billion, but because of its position, it had to settle for far less.

It was said that in addition to the hostages, the money had been sent to pay for the contracts that were cancelled when the Shaw left in 1979. Iran had been paid in cash, because it could not access the global financial systems due to international sanctions it was under at the time. At first glance, the transaction seemed legitimate. However, on closer inspection, there was a more concise reason for the money, and that was from advancing nuclear technology too quickly.

The Joint Comprehensive Plan of Action (JCPOA), or Iran nuclear deal, had been signed in Vienna on July 14, 2015 by Iran and the P5+1, which included the United States, China, France, Russia, Germany and the United Kingdom. The Pact limits Iran's nuclear program in exchange for sanctions relief. The United Nations Security Council endorsed the JCPOA Iran's nuclear program in July of 2015 and it was to run until October 2025. The JCPOA includes some of the following provisions:

Enrichment

- Iran's enrichment capacity, enrichment level and stockpile will be limited for specified directions.

- There will be no enrichment facilities other than Natanz.

- Iran is allowed to conduct research and development of centrifuges with and agreed scope and schedule.

- Fordow, the underground enrichment center will be converted to nuclear physics and technology center.

Reprocessing

- The heavy water facility in Arak with help of international venture will be re-designed and modernized to "Heavy Water Research Reactor" with no weapon grade plutonium byproducts.

- The spent fuel will be exported, there will be no re-processing.

Monitoring

- Implementation of the modified code 3.1 and provisional application of the additional protocol. Iran was given strict instructions to follow this.

Sanctions

When the IAEA verifies Iran's implementation of the key nuclear commitments:

- The EU will terminate all nuclear related economic sanctions.

- The United States will cease the application of all nuclear related secondary Economic and Financial sanctions.

The UN Security Council well endorse the agreement with a resolution that terminates all previous nuclear related resolutions and incorporate certain restrictive measures for a mutually agreed period of time.

In 2018, President Trump withdrew the United States from the deal, claiming it didn't stop Iran's missile program and original influence. In 2020, Iran said it would no longer follow the deal's limitations but would continue to work with the IAEA. In December 2020, Iranian officials said they were to join the deal if the U.S. lifted sanctions and rejoined the deal.

On October 18, 2023, all remaining nuclear related sanctions against Iran expired, including restrictions on ballistic missiles and sensitive technologies.

There are more specifications to the pacts.

The United States had sent inspectors from the Atomic Energy Commission (AEC) to Iran numerous times, since the above pacts were signed, but they could not find anything wrong. Most of the facilities were buried deep underground. The US AEC inspectors were not able to view those facilities and that's where almost all the nuclear equipment, including the centrifuges, was kept. The inspectors viewed mainly the storage facilities that kept some of the upstream nuclear equipment on the surface. We knew they were lying but to keep the peace, at least for now, we let it go. However, we had an ace, because years ago, the word was that Mossad Intel and the United States Department of Homeland Security (DHS) sent a malware called the Stuxnet virus deep into their industrial systems to disrupt Iran's nuclear program. The worm was so successful that it caused havoc and extreme delays in their plans. Its main purpose driven by Microsoft Windows was to manipulate and control the speed of centrifuges used in uranium enrichment, causing extensive damage to the nuclear infrastructure. It was the first known use of cyber terrorism.

Now a far more powerful virus called Stuxnet II has been developed by the United States and Israel and will be released to a couple of unsuspecting nations in due time.

ONE

Stuxnet Virus–2017

Jake Cannon and Slade Swanson, Delta Force Intel operatives, were sent to Iran working with the Mossad under the direct orders of the Deputy Secretary of the Department of Homeland Security James Radke, to find out how far Iran was along the path of creating a nuclear bomb. If needed, they had the expertise because along with them, they had Israeli's top nuclear scientist, Gary Zimmerman, to advance another worm into their nuclear program if warranted. The Israelis and the US had been working on another Stuxnet-like virus, since the first one. The new one was far more powerful than the original. The saving grace with this worm, developed with the help of Artificial Intelligence (AI), not only raised havoc with their centrifuges and other complex nuclear equipment but was also extremely difficult to find. It was like robbing a bank's vault and leaving without a trace. The only way to trace the malware was to use quantum mechanics software because it was so much quicker than digital software. The new software, if warranted, could catch the virus in its tracks. And it was believed that Iran did not have this capability. However, Iran was in close alliance with Russia and had been for years, and that could pose another problem. If Russia was far enough along in the development of quantum mechanics, they could lend scientists to go to Iran and inject their software into the most vulnerable areas of Iran's nuclear program and lie and wait for any worm to attack. Digital software could not identify the attack. As already stated, even staring in the face of the malware in Iran's nuclear program, it could not identify where the attack was coming from and the damage of the attack. However, Gary Zimmerman with Cannon's and Swanson's help had discovered that Iran had increased the number of centrifuges from 6,104 to their original 20,000. The 6,104 was the agreed amount that Iran and the JCPOA had negotiated on. As stated earlier, Iran dropped out of the agreement in October of 2023 and the current U.S. Administration hadn't done anything about it. It hadn't even hit the news. So now it looks like Jake and Slade will have to make a trip to Russia to see if the Russkies have developed Quantum Mechanics to the level of stopping the new malware.

TWO

Jake's Residence

Jake scratched his burnished blonde hair and hopped out of bed, rubbing his deep blue eyes. He was a big man at six foot two, very athletically built, and could hold his own against most anyone. It was 5:30 in the morning and he had time for a quick shower and a bite to eat before leaving for DHS. It was only a 45-minute drive from his house at this time of day. He lived in an old house on an acre of land on the banks of the Potomac, a few miles south of Alexandria, Virginia. He had neighbors, but not too close. He liked his privacy. He had bought the old run-down farmstead eleven years ago, right after joining DHS. The first thing he did was gut the old place and start over. The house was built in 1875 and had been remodeled twice but now it was in need of major repairs. He had done all the framing himself, including new raised ceilings and stairways. He had also upgraded the electrical and plumbing, plus installed a new roof and gutter system. Jake had hired out the painting, concrete work, and some of the finish work. A few years back he had installed all new fencing, outside lighting, and a good security system since he was away a lot. Jake enjoyed working with his hands to get his mind off of work, especially when he was vexed by complex problems. The house wasn't big by today's standard but at 3800 square feet, it was more than enough space for a bachelor.

He had some time to burn before leaving so he went out to the south side of the house where his 3500 square-foot garage was at, unlocked the side door, and walked inside. He flipped on the switches for the nine double overhead florescent lamps and admired the surroundings. The garage had an epoxy-based black and white checkered floor, but the main attraction was the five muscle cars from the 60s and early 70s, golden age of racing back. His favorite was the extremely rare 1970 shadow purple 454 cubic-inch, V8 Corvette with a Can Am RPO LS7 engine rated in stock form at 465 brake horsepower. He had driven it a few times and it had scared the bejesus out of him. Back then, the auto companies fudged on how much horsepower these cars had, in order to keep the insurance costs low for the consumer. On the dyno, the car put out 550 brake horsepower and 500ft-lbs of torque. It had taken him and his father, Michael, years to acquire the five muscle cars. The only drawback Jake could see was that they required high-octane leaded gasoline and lots of it. He checked his smart phone and it was nearly 7am–time to go.

THREE

DHS Meeting

Jake locked up the house and garage, jumped into his daily driver; a government issued Ford, and headed out. He took US 395 going north and then connected to US 66 for a short while and then continued north. He connected to Nebraska Avenue after crossing the Potomac and drove north until he got to the Nebraska Avenue Complex (NAC). He checked in at the guard post, parked his car in the parking complex, and headed to a conference room in the middle of the building.

"Good morning everyone," Jake said as he entered the large conference room.

Seated next to him was his partner in crime, Slade Swanson, and next to him sat Gary Zimmerman, the Israeli scientist who was invited to the complex by the Secretary, Mary Stinson, because of the subject matter. He was on loan from Israel. Across the table was a pretty brunette with hazel eyes by the name of Bette Briton. She was the cyber security expert keeping the teams safe while on assignment. Next to her sat Ben Larson, an expert in explosives, ammo and fire arms; very serious but always hits the mark. Next to Ben was Tom Morrison, the database and profiler expert. Across from Tom was Dr. Tonia Franks, the computer guru, and Dr. Clyde Ferris, homeland's neural net expert. The last person seated at the table was Steve Olson. His expertise (logistics) existed in the operation and control of safe houses around the globe for their agents.

Everyone stood when the Secretary of the Department of Homeland Security, Mary Stinson, came in. Ordinarily, the Deputy Secretary would conduct these meetings, but this one was of grave importance.

The Deputy Secretary, James Radke, stood and Mary motioned for him to begin. He looked in the direction of Jake and Slade and said, "This mission is of the upmost importance for you two to find out if Russia's technology in quantum mechanics is on par with ours, and if they have any plans to lend it to Iran. Heck, I want to know if they have it, and will they be lending it to anyone else."

Jake thought, just like his old boss, David Peterson. No preamble, just direct and to the point.

James looked at Jake and Slade again for a long moment before continuing. "I don't care what our administration says or does. We need to stop Russia in their tracks on this. Hell, our world is dangerous enough without this technology being spread to our enemies. You have already been briefed by Mary about this operation, but do you have any more questions now?" James asked while waving his hands around the room.

"Yes sir, I do." Jake indicated while looking at the Deputy Secretary.

"Will this operation be based only in Moscow?" Jake asked.

"Well, that all depends on what you find. You guys need to unravel this and if it leads you elsewhere, you follow. That's why we have Steve Olson here involved in this soirée." "Sir, during the preliminary briefing with Mary, it was brought up, if Russia has the same or better technology in Quantum Mechanics than we do, can we get the authority and funds to work on a virus that would disrupt their Quantum Mechanics software?" Gary Zimmerman asked.

"Gary, may I call you Gary?" The Deputy Secretary asked.

"Sure can." Gary responded.

James Radke was a small wiry man with curly brown hair and a mustache. He had been in the military and retired with the rank of Lieutenant (Light) Colonel in the Army. Like most men of his breeding and stature, he was brisk and to the point. To Jake, he was David Peterson the second–his old boss.

He continued to look in Gary's direction. "Congress didn't update the Patriot Act last time, so the act expired in 2020. However, we have other tools for the authority and acquisition of funds. Okay, you three have your airline ticket to Moscow, correct?" James asked.

"We do," Slade answered. "Couldn't we have received better accommodations on the flight, like business class?" Slade used his best impersonation of Desperado to possibly get first class from his boss. He was slightly shorter than Jake with a stocky build and wavy thick dark brown hair. But what really set him apart was his bushy eyebrows, steely black eyes and a very gravelly voice–enough to get anyone's attention.

"Afraid not." The Deputy Secretary responded. "We have you guys reserved as tourists from the get go. This time, you're in economy class."

"But why?" Slade continued.

"This is a very high priority mission and it needs to be well-covered from the time you guys step into Dulles International. Now, if there aren't any more questions, I would like to adjourn this meeting." The Deputy Secretary stood and waited for Mary to adjourn the meeting. Afterward, he looked around again and left the room.

Slade looked at Jake and asked, "Boy, James seemed all tensed up today. I'm wondering if there's something else that's causing him to be so anxious."

"Naw, I don't think so. He knows how important this operation is, and everyone at this table should also know this." Jake looked around and saw who were still there, nodding. "Okay, we got our marching orders. It's time to go home and start packing. Our flight is scheduled to leave 8:45 am tomorrow morning at Dulles International."

After arriving home, Jake took some time to relax and think about the task at hand. He already knew the process that Slade and Gary and himself would be going through. It wasn't so different that he and the others went through to learn the machinations of other missions. He knew this meeting was very important because Mary Stinson was there.

His eyes started to grow heavy and he decided to take a nap on his couch.

FOUR

Moscow

The Aeroflot landed at the Shermetyevo International Airport on time, and without incident during the long flight. The Boeing 777 flew northeast over the north pole and took slightly more than eleven hours and landed at 8:45pm, Moscow time. The airport was the oldest of the four International airports serving Moscow. It was converted into a civilian airport in 1959 and is now the eighth busiest airport in Europe. Getting through security was more rigid than the United States. All three of them got through as tourists and each had a thirty day visa. Jake was wondering if they made it through too easily, and told Slade and Gary to be on their best behavior and be cautious. The weather wasn't too bad for this time of year with a slate gray sky and light snow fall. Nevertheless, early November could turn on its tracks and bring bitter cold weather from the Northeast. DHS had six safe houses scattered throughout the city and they were directed to the Central District where most of the administrative business were done. This was the oldest part of the city where the Kremlin and Red Square resided. Who would have thought that DHS had a safe house right in the lion's den?

After unpacking, they took the day of familiarizing themselves with the surrounding area, and where the secondary safe house was in case the circumstances warranted them to leave quickly. Afterward they all met in the kitchen to discuss their plan. Gary had a friend that lived in one of the beautiful apartment buildings along Tverskaya Street. It was one of Moscow's thoroughfares that was emblematic of its history. His friend was also a nuclear scientist and had connections with the State Duma. The Duma wield immense political power not unlike our congress. Gary's friend, Yuri Dubrovsky, worked for The Russian Academy of Sciences (RAS), and more specifically for Budker Institute of Nuclear Physics. Normally, Yuri, would be working at the institute in the Siberian town of Akademgorodok. However, this year, Yuri was able to get a year's sabbatical in Moscow and was fortunate enough to get a place along Tverskaya Street from his friend in the Duma.

The information about where the correct building was located that contained the equipment for the quantum mechanics and computing software was already in the mail slot of the house when they arrived. Yuri had already deposited the data an hour before they arrived. He made sure it was the correct safe house before the deposit. The operatives were on a strict time schedule because of the importance of the operation.

Moscow State University MSU) was their target and one of the leaders in quantum theory and mechanics. And as far as Yuri knew, the school had the most advanced information and theory on the science. The Director of Computer Science, Mikhail Novikov, at Moscow State University of Instrument Engineering and Computer Science was a renowned scientist in the field. Mikhail attended and spoke at numerous conferences around the world, and this is where Yuri met and became fast friends with him. Gary Zimmerman also attended some of the same conferences and met both Mikhail and Yuri. Between the three, they had universal knowledge of not only Nuclear Physics but also Quantum Mechanics and Computing. Gary and Yuri also published a paper together on Nuclear Fusion.

After getting the information from the mail slot, and reconnoitering the surrounding area and then going through the details of the plan a second time they were now ready to travel to Moscow State University the next day. After breakfast, Jake had the unceremonious duty of cleaning up before leaving. The university was located a fifteen minute walk from their apartment. But before they left for MSU Jake and Slade needed a basic primer (White Papers) introduction to quantum computing.

FIVE

Quantum Computing I

"Do you guys have your heads on, because even at the basic level it is quite complicated?" Gary asked. Jake and Slade looked at each other and shrugged. Jake was the first to speak.

"Yeah, Slade and I were briefly introduced to it while stopping a group of terrorist from using it against our financing and taxing authorities a few years ago."

""Well, I guess a good starting point is nanotechnology. We need to start here because the realm quantum computing works in is an unimaginably small environment. Nano technology has opened up new frontiers in all sciences and affects our everyday lives in ways we wouldn't have thought possible. Nano machines hold promise for a myriad of commercial and military applications. For instance, these tiny nano engines working on a nano, pico and even femto magnitudes can hold such small information packets that the entire contents of the Library of Congress can be stored in an area no larger than a sugar cube. Gary looked at the two operatives and asked are you still with me?" They both nodded.

"I'm giving you a wide area of basic understanding of this science so when we actually get to quantum computing you will be able to understand it more easily. Because of this, medical science can now create very tiny devices with designer cells based on one's DNA that can travel through the human body, targeting and killing clusters of cancer cells before they can spread to other parts of the body."

Gary went on to say, that he had researched both DNA and quantum computing and found that even though DNA computers have very fast processing speeds to solve a wide array of medical problems, he chose quantum computing because it was particularly adept at solving large mathematical factoring problems and algorithms that are used in cryptography. And this knowledge was pushed even faster by artificial intelligence.

Gary saw that Jake had questions. "I'll get to AI later when needed." Gary said.

Jake and Slade just looked at Gary as if he was some kind of god.

"I thought you are a nuclear engineer." Jake said.

"I am, but I also have a PhD in Quantum Mechanics and the field really fascinates me." Gary answered.

SIX

Digital Certification and Computing

"**N**ow where was I, oh yes, cipher keys are at the heart of digital certification. Most cipher keys are based on very large prime numbers and in number theory. Prime factorization is the disassembling of composite numbers into lessor non-trivial divisors, which when multiplied together equal the original number. You guys still with me?" Gary asked.

"I think so." Slade said. "In a nut shell, you are saying that digital computing is based on the ciphers containing very large prime numbers, in order to stop intrusions at the gateways of systems. Is that right?" Slade asked with his steely black eyes in heavy concentration.

"Very good, Slade." Gary responded. "I guess you guys are pretty smart after all." "Yup." They both responded.

"Well now we are building quantum machines that are capable of 500 sextillion floating-point operations per second (500 zettaflops) and when we get there we will essentially render digital security on the Internet useless."

"Wow!" exclaimed the intel ops.

"But first we need to construct tiny nano and quantum machines that will enable us to produce ever-faster quantum computers with the help of AI. Now let's get down to visual cues that will aid you to understand what I'm talking about. Let's compare quantum computing to digital computing,"

Gary put a ball and a coin on the table and went on. "We all know that digital computing has two discreet states of zero and one just like two sides of a coin. You flip the coin and you have the other state. When you link these states (bits) together called bytes in the form of binary code, these structures are instructions for the Central Processing Unit

(CPU). The CPU can handle bytes in the form of 4 bits per second. Larger CPU's for mainframes and super computers can handle up to sixty-four bits per second. And some now can handle one-hundred and twenty-eight bits per second. These bytes are called instructions or data sets as I said, and these are all in the form of binary code. However, if you want faster processing you can link mainframes or super computer together. Say you wanted to get 640 bits per second on a 64 bit machine, and then you would link 10 machines together. Pretty easy to understand, right?" Gary ask.

"Sure is." Both intel ops agreed. "But how many of these computers can you link together?" Slade ask, while rubbing his fingers through his thick coal black hair.

"Well, let's look it up." Gary responded. "It says here that supercomputers can contain tens of thousands of nodes that can work together to solve problems using interconnect communication. These nodes can also use interconnects to communicate with I/O systems, like networking and data storage. Pretty fast huh guys."

"Yeah, you would think so." Jake said shaking his head in wonder.

SEVEN

Quantum Computing II

"Now, let's get to the fun part known as quantum computing. This is an entirely different animal, if you will," Gary said.

"When you roll a ball across the table you have quaternary states called qubits of zero or zero and one, or a supposition of both. In other words a qubit in its pure state can be represented as a linear combination of zero and one. You can look at that combination as being in two states simultaneously, or as an example, a light switch with a dimmer shows various states of being on and off at the same time. Each one of those states or chain of states can be interpreted as sets of instructions that go to the quantum computer processors. Are you still with me?" Gary asked. He could now see that they were both grappling with the concepts.

"Never mind for now," Gary said. "Wait until I'm done with the explanations, then I will answer any questions you may have."

He looked in the direction of the intel ops and could see they were nodding their heads. Gary further stated by opening the doors to processing at the molecular level and harnessing the power of the atom's natural energy using ions, photons and electrons without the tedious task of constructing parallel processors in the classical sense, you can increase processing speeds exponentially. *Besides*, he thought, *we are approaching the boundary in the digital world using Moore's law.* Gary went on to state that Gordon E Moore, co-founder of Intel, in his 1965 paper had noted that the number of integrated circuits will double every year or so since the invention of these circuits in 1958 till around 2020 or so when they approach the size of atoms. At this point the era of integrated circuits etched on silicon wafers will end. So far the era has been extended by the use of new materials, but will end quite soon. Gary continued his discussion on quantum mechanics and elucidated on the issues of measurement and entanglements in quantum physics. He stated you first must find a way to accurately measure the qubit states of one or more sub atomic particles without collapsing to the value that is measured.

"Hold on, guys. I'll be done soon and then I'll answer any questions you might have. Hopefully, to make this clearer, if one measures the state (spin, motion and harmonics) of an atom, one or more neighboring atoms will take on the characteristics of the atom being measured. Such systems are said to be in an entangled state if it cannot be written as a tensor product of its constituent subsystems. We eventually solved this problem by using a new type of photonic crystal laser to individually measure the spin, motion and harmonics of each sub atomic particle and groups of sub atomic particles without artificially altering the decay of its orbit, motion, and harmonics and without changing its neighboring atoms or sub atomic particles' characteristics. While part of our team was overcoming the barriers of super position, entanglement, distance, measurement and how to build quantum machines that would aid them in constructing faster quantum computers, another team of quantum scientists were addressing the issues of developing environments to control the interactions between sub atomic particles, and how to build nano machines that would enable them to send nano packets of electromagnetic energy to digital computers' information systems. We had known that any form of energy could be transformed into another form and in all such energy processes, including total input, output and the exchange mechanism was equal to the total amount of energy in a closed system. In the case of quantum mechanics when using electromagnetic energy, the electromagnetic wave of these states are called quanta of light or photons, and the electromagnetic radiation field could control these sub atomic particles by regulating the voltage in the field.

Another method was to lower the environment's temperature close to zero degrees Kelvin (absolute zero) in order to control the atoms' interactions. In other words, these particles needed to be aligned in recognizable patterns such as strings to facilitate their measurements.

So in the end, it was decided to use atomic units of photons controlled within an electromagnetic field. We determined that we could generate enough electromagnetic energy through high-powered capacitors to create a strong enough field to control the sub atomic photons while at the same time boost the electromagnetic energy to the nano packets. For testing, we set up our own botnet with firewalls that had very sophisticated gateway cipher keys based on Shor's quantum algorithm for integer factorization. The new quantum computer running at nearly 400 zettaflops took less than five minutes to crack the prime factors of very large semiprimes. This of course will render the internet useless using digital computers and digital gateways. We can now decipher the gateways and send nano packets of electromagnetic energy through the interior systems and subsystem like a pack of hungry wolves, destroying the software and back out without a trace and, more dangerously, alter the software with our algorithms and leave no one the wiser. Of course, our quantum computers are running much faster now than our initial testing.

"You guys have a pretty good handle on this?" Gary asked, while taking off his glasses to clean them.

They both nodded and Jake said, "Gary, this is the second time we have encountered this and thank God for the additional training. I know our lives could depend on this basic knowledge. Slade and I are grateful for this."

"Well, I'm glad I could help, because if we get stopped, and I know we will probably get detained more than once, there is a chance you may be asked a few basic questions about quantum computing. I believe you now have enough knowledge to pass their questions. As you know, we have to present ourselves as a small group of bumbling Russian quantum scientists and engineers who have lost their way."

EIGHT

Hijinks Of
The Highest Order

All three casually looked around as they were approaching MSU grounds. Even though they had satellite, stock photos and intimate knowledge from Yuri, it was quite intimidating. They had authentic looking Russian credentials in case they were stopped and asked to identify themselves, and they knew they would. The first trip to MSU was on foot to case out the place as best they could from the street, and to figure out the best place to park their car on a later visit. They knew they had to get to one of the interior parking lots in front of the quantum labs to do the operation. This in itself was a daunting task, because of the design and size of the campus. There was a small lake in front of some of the labs and one of those was for quantum mechanics and computing. Gary's friend, Yuri, was back from MSU's extension school in Siberia for a sabbatical as noted earlier, and had helped them to identify the building that had the equipment containing the datum they needed to extract.

The thumb drives they had were not ordinary. They looked ordinary and contained 500 megs for each drive. Instead of inserting information they extracted data. Each one had algorithms embedded in them to store the needed data. Artificial Intelligence (AI) also played a role here. Once through the gateways, it instructed the software where to look, and the easiest and shortest route to get to the information they were seeking. And the sticks were extremely fast; they had to be because they were based on quantum mechanics. Once in, they needed the quickness and accuracy of the sticks, lest they get caught red-handed. All of them knew what that meant. There would be no way for the U.S. to negotiate their release and most likely they would be tortured and sent to the gulags in Siberia forever, if not outright execution! Another highlight of the extraction was once completed, all original code was put back in its proper place and sequence, including any flags that were changed during the theft. No one would be the wiser!

From the outside looking in, and from Gary's friend's instructions, they determined the shortest route and possible check points they had to maneuver to get to the right parking lot with their car. With the satellite photos to also aid them, it gave them confidence they would be on the right track. They had to be or the gulag had their names in brass.

NINE

Strategy

After arriving back to their apartment and eating a fine meal, they sat down and rolled out an old-fashioned detailed map of the MSU campus and compared it to an online internet map and satellite photos. They already knew most of the checkpoints from Gary's friend's discussion. Ordinarily, a good many of Russia's college campuses had minimum security and no checkpoints, but universities with sensitive data is a whole different animal. MSU with a full complement of the physical sciences including quantum mechanics was heavily guarded with multiple layers of increasing security. They already knew, in this case, there were three layers of security. The first layer was mainly for checking credentials. The next two required Yuri's okay to let them through. However, the third one was information intensive and required substantial knowledge of who they were, what they were doing and who they were seeing. At this point they needed to know the knowledge of the lab(s) they were visiting.

They intently studied all three documents in order to determine if there were any loop holds, and they did find two weaknesses in the MSU layers of security. The first one involved changing shifts at the check point. First off, the shifts were all changed at the same time at all check points which presented a double edged sword. Second, during the change each security guard coming on shift was somewhat distracted by the fact that they had to read an updated daily report. Studying each report took about ten to fifteen minutes of their time. This created a huge distraction of their duties and would provide a good time for the three of them to check in. Going back to the double edged sword. If the shifts were staggered this could provide time for the team to find a hiding place before timing their move to the next security point. All in all they were glad that the shift change occurred at the same time. If they were prepared enough it would minimize the drama, and teams like these hated drama. Drama could lead to mistakes and the likelihood to a Siberian gulag. The team would drive a Lada Vista, a Russian auto when it was time to infiltrate MSU.

"Gary, do you think the Lada is appropriate for the team to be driving?" Jake asked, rubbing his hands together.

Gary thought for a minute while looking at the Delta Force soldiers before answering. "The Lada is, of course, Russian made and quite economical. For us, the car is perfect for our appearance. Russian scientists and engineers don't make a good salary so we drive cheap cars. Although if we need a quick exit, the auto will fail miserably. So let's hope our plan goes off without a hitch."

After the round table, everyone went and gathered and organized their gear for tomorrow's intrusion. They needed to hit the sack early in order to be bright-eyed and bushy-tailed for tomorrows's main event. Besides, there wasn't anything else to talk about.

TEN

Intrusion

No one, including the operatives, could carry firearms or any metal-based weapons inside the MSU campus. This, of course, was for security reasons. However, this gave the operatives an advantage, especially for the likes of Jake and Slade because of their extensive training that turned them into natural born killers. And they were packing. Some of technology they used was a step back in some ways, but highly effective especially in the hands of killers like the Delta Force operatives. They used Polycarbonate Ceramic knives and hand guns made out of high tensile strength materials to get past the magnetometers at the security posts. The ammo they used was basically like dry ice and made from a new material that was nearly as dense as lead and was programmable. It was referred to as smart bullets because of its characteristics. The bullets could be programmed in various ways. It could miss most civilians and children when fighting in areas that had high density of that kind. It could be programmed to a person's DNA and within 600 meters the bullet will find and kill that individual. Yes, it will go around corners, through windows, or any obstacles to get at its target. The science is similar to guided missiles but on a more personal basis. The beauty of the technology is after it finds its prize it evaporates like dry ice and no trace is left for ballistics. And there are no casings!

"Is everyone ready? Jake asked as the Lada approached the MSU campus. Everyone nodded. "Okay, we'll place old fashion C4 explosives at the entrance and in other areas we see fit. Slade and I will remotely discharge them if needed."

"If there is an explosion, how long will it take armed security to arrive?" Gary asked.

Jake looked at Slade to answer Gary's question since he was well-versed in this area and could give the nuclear scientist a more precise answer. "There is already some armed security on location, but only a very few. Also, this is their Unity Day, which signifies the end of the Polish occupation of Moscow in 1612, and the Time of Troubles. And like most nations, they celebrate their holidays heartily. In Russia's case, you add great quantities of their national drink, vodka, and…you see where I'm going with this. Yes, additional security will eventually show up but more times than not, on this occasion, they will be drunk and confused."

"Look smartly, everyone. We are approaching the first security post. You're up, Gary," Jake quipped. The post looked dirty with a lot of cans and wrappers around. The guard stepped out and approached the car.

Gary said hello in Russian to the guard. The guard greeted Gary and then looked past him to the other two fellows and they both nodded their heads as they were handing their credentials to Gary. He handed the guard each person's credential and waited for the guard to hand it back before handing him another set. The guard asked the basic questions on who you are going to see and if they were enjoying their stay in Russia. After Gary received back all the credentials, the guard pointed them on.

Gary put the car in gear and drove on. They drove a short distance on the main road then turned left to go to the next security outlet. Here they were greeted by another guard that seemed somewhat distracted by his daily update sheet, and probably suffering from a hangover. However, he snapped to while questioning the car's occupants. After inspecting their credentials the soldier instructed all three occupants of the Lada to step out so he could thoroughly inspect the car, including the glove box and the small trunk. The operatives were surprise about this, but nevertheless let the soldier do his duty. They were very compliant to the guard's request. Gary asked direction to the next outpost that would eventually guide them to the physical science complex of buildings that contained the information they were after. To break the tension, Gary even joked to the guard that they were glad they were not carrying rocket launchers. After the inspection, the soldier slapped a small sticker on the car to indicate that it was already inspected. He then saluted them and pointed in the direction of the next security shack that they needed to go, in order to reach the physical science complex of buildings. While driving there, Jake checked the guard's direction on a small device he was carrying to be sure. Everything matched. Afterward, Jake and Slade hid their weapons and devices in a concealed area of the car that was easy to reach if needed. They were pretty sure that they would be searched at the third outpost.

As they approached the guard shack Gary was boisterous, talking in Russian, to Jake and Slade in hopes that the guard overheard some of this. While Jake and Slade were nodding and laughing at Gary, he said hello in Russian, to the soldier. After greeting each other the guard instructed them to step out of the car so he could do a quick inspection of the auto, check their credentials and then search all three of them. The soldier then asked some basic scientific questions from a script to all three of them. Gary apologized to the guard that his comrades were too drunk to effectively answer some of the questions, because they celebrated the holiday too heartily. The guard and Gary laughed about this and the soldier then told him that he wasn't doing too well himself. After getting directions to the complex from the guard, Gary put the Lada in gear and drove to their destination.

ELEVEN

The Complex

When they arrived and parked next to an old Mercedes in the lot next to the blue building, Jake checked the directions from Yuri and they were spot on. They got out of the Lada one by one and checked their electronic key cards that they got from Yuri and walked toward the red entrance of the blue building, known as big blue without saying a word. They casually looked around and saw that there wasn't anything out of place. Gary inserted the key card in the slot on the red door entrance and waited for the click, to see if Yuri was truly a good friend–he was. They all walked into the lobby and looked around and saw there was a guard post in the center of the lobby. Oh, oh, they all whispered in unison–Yuri didn't mention this! They walked up to the security post and Gary greeted the guard in Russian and showed her his security badge that opened the door. She nodded and asked for the other two badges. She briefly inspected the other two badges and with a smile like a Hollywood starlet, she waved them through the glass partition.

"Boy what a knockout," Jake whispered. "If I had more time I would go a round or two with her. Hey guys did you see what she was wearing? If that's an official Russian security uniform–bring it on!"

Slade just shook his and for the zillionth time and said, "buddy don't you ever give up?"

"Heck no, why should I do that?" Jake quipped. They both could hear Gary chuckling in the background.

Slade knew that Jake was a consummate bachelor and probably would never change. He lived by himself along the banks of the Potomac in a comfortable home on an acre of land. Deep down he knew in his heart and soul Jake was a real gear head and wouldn't change his ways of tinkering and racing his muscle cars. He had five of them sitting on a checkered black and white glossy floor in his huge garage. He wanted

Jake's 67 purple haze Chevy Nova. He asked his friend more than once about buying the car and the only answer he received from him was why would he want to upset the ratio of women to cars and grinned.

Slade's outlook toward the world was totally different than his friend. He was a divorced father with two wonderful daughters, Marla and Darla. He always felt he got the shaft from his former wife when she walked out on him to see if the grass was greener on the other side and it wasn't! She had the gall to come back a year later and wanted back in. During that year he went through hell and the only thing that saved him was working on the house non-stop whenever he got the chance, and this experience changed him forever. He told her no, and he was sure that this changed her forever. *"Hell has no fury like a woman scorned."* Sure, he loved his daughters, but now his allegiance was to his government career and to his country.

Gary moved between the two operatives and whispered, "its zero time fellas, and we have to get this done quickly. Do you remember what the term Gulag means?" They both nodded.

Gary led them down a narrow corridor to a bank of elevators, picked one and hit two on the brass plate and they waited for the car to arrive They stepped off onto the second floor and went down another narrow corridor until they arrived at a glass door with lettering indicating they were at the right place. Gary entered his key card in the slot next to the door and waited for the all-encompassing sound of click to happen, and it was music to his ears. He thought, *now we're getting someplace.* He whispered to the two Delta Force operatives to take their post in the large room as previously deemed. Gary took out the three thumb drives and headed to the back wall where a banked and arrayed interconnected nodes stood at attention. He first had to take out a special key that Yuri gave him to unlock the cover. He studied the rows of nodes and finally determined where he needed to insert the first I/O drive into the USB port. He waited for it to finish and was shocked how fast the theft was completed. He now wasn't sure if he completed the instructions correctly that Yuri provided. He didn't have time to dither, so he walked over to another bank of nodes as instructed and inserted the second drive, and again it finished lightning fast. He thought when he got home he would have to look up the engineer that created these drives. He was duly impressed. *Like a pack of vicious and hungry wolves,* he thought. He came out from the rows of nodes and indicated to the two ops to follow him to the next room so he could insert the last thumb drive. *So far so good,* he thought. The enclosure was further down the corridor from the last room they were in. Again, Gary inserted his key card into the slot next to the glass door and it opened. They walked in quietly, and Jake and Slade took up their posts while Gary moved to another bank of nodes against the far wall. He noticed the room was colder than the other enclosure and wondered why. *Oh well,* he thought, *this is it,* and unlocked the array cover and inserted the last I/O drive into the USB port. Just then Gary and the two operatives heard footsteps rushing down the corridor toward them.

TWELVE

Staying Alive

"**Q**uick, hide in place until we know what's going on," Jake whispered.

"But where?" Gary asked.

"Be creative. Anywhere here but out of sight," Slade said.

Gary looked around and saw some cabinets and rushed over to them and opened one of the doors and luckily saw some space. He muttered, *what the hell,* and crawled in and closed the cupboard door. *He was glad that he was small for a change,* he thought again.

Slade came around the corner and looked at Jake. "Let's move it," Jake said. "Stand next to the entrance door and be ready."

The operatives waited with their smart weapons drawn and followed the sound as the footsteps raced past them. Jake waited 30 seconds and didn't hear any more sounds. He carefully opened the glass door and looked both ways and saw nothing and whispered to Slade to get Gary. After Gary and Slade arrived at the door, the three of them moved quickly down the hall to the nearest bank of elevators. Jake took out the electronic map device he was carrying and dialed up the buildings schematics to check all feasible escape routes. There weren't many. They exited the elevator on the first floor and rushed past the security post. Jake looked back at the pretty blonde with a startled look on her face as she reached for the phone. They moved down the steps to their car and Jake stopped suddenly and looked at the old Mercedes parked next to the Lada.

"We're going in the Mercedes, guys. It's built like a tank and much faster than the Lada. The thing we need now more than anything else is speed." Slade and Gary both nodded. He took off his coat and wrapped it around his arm and popped the driver side window and watched as it disintegrated into a cloud of silver smoke. He slid in and took his ceramic knife and separated the steering column to get at the ignition wires.

He touched them together and the old beast fired up. Just as Slade and Gary were coming around the other side, security busted through the entrance of the building and fired their handguns at them. Jake reached out through the cleared window and fired at the soldiers as Slade slid into the front passenger seat while Gary took the backseat. Jake put the car in gear and sped out of the parking lot like there was no tomorrow. Bullets ricocheted off the trunk of the Mercedes, and one found its mark as the back window caved in.

Slade turned to Gary and yelled, "You okay?"

"Sure am, but scared out of my mind." Gary responded.

"Don't worry, Jake will get us out of this mess."

By now, Jake was putting distance between them and security as a large black car came out of nowhere and was chasing them. He showed no mercy to the old Mercedes as he was racing it like one of his muscle cars. Grit was flying on the wings of testosterone as he wheeled the car toward the main entrance. He could see soldiers were barricading it, but he was driving a tank for a car and was confident that he could break through. With a horrific screech he slammed through as the old car, taking more bullets, raced on. He skidded left, smoking the big Mercedes rear tires and fish tailed violently as he gain traction on the thoroughfare away from the front gate and raced through neighborhoods escaping their assailants. After a reckless five minutes that would confuse anyone in a maze, Jake parked the riddled old Mercedes and hailed a cab to take them part way back to their apartment. Gary asked why they were so far away from their residence?

"We'll discard our coats as we walk back in order to give us better cover," Slade answered. "You understand?" Slade asked.

"Yeah, it makes sense. You guys know what you're doing." Gary responded.

They walked back in silence now as the two ops were on high alert for anything out of the ordinary.

THIRTEEN

Playing God With More Quantum

After arriving back to their apartment half frozen, Slade grabbed some paper, kindling and wood from the wood box and started a fire. Gary wanted more heat quickly so he turned up the thermostat. After getting comfortable they sat around the kitchen table to see what they had. Before getting down to business. Gary asked about the Lada they left in the parking lot.

"Don't worry buddy," Jake said with a smile. "With the credentials we left in renting the junker, officials will be chasing their tails for some time before they discover it's a ruse."

Slade, chuckled seeing the relief on Gary's face.

Gary, slipped the first drive into his USB port on his laptop and muttered my, my.

"What's going on?" Jake queried in all sincerity.

"Well what I'm reading here, at least on the first drive, it seems that Russia is rather secretive in allowing artificial intelligence (AI) to be shared with other entities. It stifles their advancement in Quantum Mechanics and Computing–good for us." Gary said.

"How so," Slade questioned, his gravelly voice trailing off.

Gary thought for a moment before he answered, "what I'm seeing here reminds me of a closed distributed bot system. It's analogous to information being shared by only a few entities within a ringed closed environment sharing their own gateway passwords, flags and other obstacles to get at the datum. If you don't have the keys, you can't get in. This is tantamount to very tight security, but impedes their advancement in allowing AI to help them advance Quantum Mechanics and Nano technology. I'm not inferring that they shouldn't protect their sensitive information and they should, but they are not allowing hordes of software engineers and programmers to advance AI in an open system. In essence, you need all three technologies working in harmony to advance Quantum Computing at a good rate, plus you need break throughs."

"It looks like Russia has not completely left the cold war philosophy," Jake said.

"It seems so," Gary interjected. "As you know, we have left a little present for our comrades. We know the first Stuxnet virus deleted most of the code and systems for Iran's nuclear program. This put their dreams of entering the nuclear brotherhood back at least ten years. In this case, Iran pretty much knew that it was Mossad that released the worm." Gary gave it a moment for this to sink in to the two operatives, and thought about how he was going to phrase his next statement. "Stuxnet II is far more advanced and devious then the original code. This time the back of Stuxnet II ups the game of Quantum Mechanics. Even though we haven't found a reliable Quantum hard drive yet, we are getting much closer. In the old 1D structure of keeping the qubits in a single line to enable quantum computation on the molecular level using either Electromagnetism or Kelvin near zero technology, we spent most of the energy of keeping these qubits in a row to do our computations. However, the entanglement rate was one to one-thousand whereas it should be at least one to one-trillion. So in effect we have a ways to go. But with our new technology onboard now, we are moving closer to understanding climate, long range weather patterns, medical break throughs and a host of other problems."

Gary paused for a long moment to gather his thoughts as to what he was going to say next. "Okay guys, I'll tell you a portion of the breakthrough we just made in order to give you a better understanding on how this all works."

Jake and Slade could only nod their heads at the scientist.

"There have been a couple of scientist in Sydney, Australia that have created a three dimensional model on the molecular level scaling a lattice structure within this structure to provide the backbone on how qubits are positioned. They then scale a 2 dimension correction model layered within the 3 D model to greatly decrease the error rate of entanglements. Measurements have shown that the entangle rate is now one in one-hundred million instead of one in one-thousand. In essence this has made quantum computing much faster. Most of the energy now is for computing not for correcting entanglements. We have modeled this new technology into the Stuxnet II virus. This time the strike of Stuxnet II will be like a pack of vicious and hungry dire wolves getting past their gateways, switches, routers and servers and the like in the blink of an eye. This time the holder of the code (worm), which is Russia, will be left betwixt and befuddled as to what happened–if it happens. You have to remember Russia is a far more dangerous adversary than Iran. We have to be careful not to ruffle Mother Russia's feathers too much, lest we are looking at the possibility of World War III."

FOURTEEN

God May Be Taking Lessons

"**H**ow does it really work?" Slade asked in a very earnest tone, using his gravelly voice to full effect.

Gary thought again for a long moment to gather his thoughts. *After the breakthrough and the modeling, he and the Israeli Mossad were in love with the frightening power of the new virus. It was really equal to the power of the Hydrogen Bomb. Together with its speed, power and ferocity, the code is a symphony of how mankind can be harnessed and confused generated by the extreme power of three advanced technologies working together in unison. It's beautiful, but at the same time deadly.* "How would you love to be embraced by a beautiful Valentine mistress and then brutally knifed and killed without ever knowing it? It can possibly control and destroy nations without firing a single bullet or exploding a single bomb."

"What?!!!" the two soldiers huffed together.

"Sorry, guys. I was thinking some of this out loud of what this code can do. Anyway, I'll tell you this virus can be unleashed anytime, anyplace in the world remotely once its inserted. Also, we can release certain parts of the code without activating other sections. And if needed we can retreat the active code."

"What do you mean by all this?" Jake asked while looking at his partner's face showing incredulity.

"It's called compartmentalization. We can back out portions of the code with our catch and replace the original code as if nothing happened. To further drive home the point it's actually a symphony of all its parts. It's like playing in an orchestra and using certain instruments if we wish to get the desired tone. Of course. you have to realize this is quantum code, not digital code or sheet music. The speed of which it can attack or retract is light years ahead of its brethren. If we want, we now can write and insert similar code to attack any infrastructure in the world."

"Oh my God!" Jake exclaimed. "You're inferring that it has human qualities. You guys are playing with fire. You know that?"

"Yeah, it's so sophisticated it can self-learn way beyond human boundaries if we're not careful. However, we can place roadblocks, barriers if you will, in parts of the code to minimize this danger. The reason for the self-learning aspect is: as it goes through an alien system it needs to learn the clearest and shortest path to get at its prize. We use all types of tools to maximize these skills, such as decision tree and critical path analysis. Of course, the tools we use depends on the type of systems we attack, and what we are after."

"I sure hope so, because if you're not careful mankind could be in jeopardy."

"Don't you know that I know that?" Gary exclaimed.

By now Jake could see the gleam in Gary's eyes. "So this little drive you have is out of this world as far as power. My God, you have to be crazy using such power, you know that!" Jake exclaimed. "You're practically playing God with His toys from His arsenal." Just then, they heard a knock on the door.

FIFTEEN

Yuri

Slade hustled Gary to another room while Jake went to the front door. He peaked through the small glass opening in the middle of the door and breathed a sigh of relief seeing it was Yuri. He was still cautious though while opening the door and looked around before greeting him. "Hey, come in, Yuri." Jake said with a smile. Jake closed the door and yelled at Slade to bring Gary back into the living room. Gary and Yuri embraced and said their hellos.

"You seem troubled." Gary said to his friend.

Yuri looked at the two Delta Force ops before speaking. "I just spoke with a comrade of mine and he indicated that there is a manhunt in progress looking for you three. Because of the nature of the situation this has gone clear up the chain. In addition to the regular police agencies the Federal Security Service (FSB) is involved. You guys need to figure a way of getting out now," Yuri said in an agitated voice.

"Now, hold on, Yuri," Jake intoned in a calm voice. "By now all avenues of escape are closed. It would be stupid for us to leave now."

"I suppose so," Yuri replied. "What will you do?"

"It's better you know nothing about our plans, in case you get questioned, " Jake cautioned.

"God, I hope I won't get questioned!" Yuri bemoaned. "I'll fall apart!"

"No, you won't." Jake continued in a calm but cautious voice. "You know about the gulags, don't you? Just go about your business as usual and if there is a chance you get detained act surprised. You'll be okay."

Gary looked at his friend. "Jake's right you know. But now you must leave and forget that you ever came here. We'll be alright."

Yuri said his goodbyes and left.

Jake studied Gary for a moment and asked, "Will Yuri be okay?"

"Ya he'll be fine."

"You sure'" Jake answered his own question. "We'll be closing up shop now." He looked at Slade. "Make the call now." Slade got on the sat phone and with encryption on he made the call to DHS.

Slade turned to Gary and said, "We'll be leaving in a couple of hours so let's clean this place up and leave no evidence behind."

"Where are we going?" Gary quizzed with a frown on his narrow face.

"Never mind, just pack up. Jake and I will take care of the rest."

SIXTEEN

New Digs

After Slade made the call, Jake conferred with him to get the details on how the State Department would handle this. The Delta Force ops always needed to be on the same page when on assignment.

"Well buddy I talked to James Radke first because of the nature of the situation and he transferred me to Steve Olson. Steve is now in the process of sending a state car camouflage as a Russian cab. The car will be here in about 30 minutes."

"In the meantime, buddy, we have to go through this place with a fine tooth comb. We can't even leave a human hair. I think the vision of a gulag will ensure that."

They both chuckled as Gary came into the room with his suitcase. "What's so funny fellas?"

"Just a private joke between us jokers." Jake intoned.

"When's the car coming?" Gary asked.

"About 20 minutes." Jake answered as Slade went into Gary's room to do a twice over.

When Slade came out they sat in silence, each wrapped in their own thoughts until the cab arrived. After the black colored cab showed up the ops stowed the suit cases in the trunk. Jake got into the front while Slade and Gary slid into the back. The driver motioned Jake to open the glove box. "Well looky here," Jake said with a smile. He reached back and handed Slade a Heckler and Koch 45 cal. with two extra 10 round mags.

"Now where talking." Slade said.

"Do we need those?" Gary commented.

"You bet your sweet bibby we do." Jake turned momentarily and looked at Gary. "As far as the Russian authorities are concerned we're a hot commodity now."

The State driver wheeled the cab through the streets of Moscow like he had a hundred time before–never even needed GPS. After a 90 minute trip they arrived at the new safe house on the outskirts of Moscow. Jake figured they were in the Northeast quadrant of the city. As the driver pulled the cab into the single garage, snow paid its presence. Even though it was early November, it wasn't unusual by Moscow standards. After retrieving their suitcases and climbing a short flight of stairs from the inside of the garage, they entered the back of the house. At this point, Ernie introduced himself to the two Delta Force ops and the scientist. Jake and Slade looked around and saw that their new digs where larger and more stately than their other place. After Ernie showed them their rooms, they met back in the living room and Gary put his laptop on the coffee table, opened it, and placed the second drive into one of the USB ports. Ernie made a fire and then made himself scarce.

SEVENTEEN

A Piece of Thumb Two

While sitting around a large round table in the big well-appointed kitchen of the safe house., Gary elucidate to his friends as to what he was seeing. "They still have a closed distributed bot environment from what I can gather on the second thumb drive." Something in what he was seeing in the code abruptly changed his course and was reminded of the United States old IRS system before it changed after the debacle twelve years ago." Speaking of which, the tax authority hasn't changed the volume of the tax code. In 1955 it was 1500 pages and today it's at least 7800 pages. I don't think there is an IRS accountant alive that understands the code in its entirety. I wonder if DOGE or any of the cabinet agencies under the new administration will reduce the size of the IRS and there voluminous code.? I know they will greatly reduce regulations and the permit process. This should really reduce the time it takes to get a new project off the ground and complete it.

Will get back to this stuff later; I have a lot to say about it. Now getting back to their quantum code. It looks good so far. There is commonality and self-learning aspects to their programming like ours, but once again I see the same problems that I saw with the contents of the first stick. They are so plagued in secrecy they cannot get over their feet. And because of this they are shooting themselves in the foot. The design of their system is first rate like ours—cool"

The two operatives look at each other and shook their heads. It seems that Gary is giving credit where credit isn't due.

"What's so cool about this?" Jake asked still looking at Slade.

"Oh, I'm sorry guys, I was thinking that on some level, they are on the same page as we are. And this brings up an interesting question. Have they copied some of our designs?

Perhaps they have gotten some of this from China or themselves. After all the previous administration let China fly so-called weather balloons over Alaska, Canada and the continental United States near some of our military bases. Further, they allowed China to purchase large swaths of land near some of our military installations.

"Don't you think we all know this," Slade huffed. "Weather balloons my ass!"

"Let's settle down everyone. We don't know if China will be a player in the mix yet, and in all probability, if it does happen, it will not happen for quite some time. We hope," Jake said.

"Now let's do a further trek into China to slake our knowledge. We now see enough evidence that China has been aiding and abetting Russia, for quite some time. However, we well have to open proper channels with them through our resources in the United State. This will take time, and in the meantime we'll be concentrating our efforts on Russia and Iran. Now let's get to the task at hand." Gary instructed.

EIGHTEEN

The Fission Scenario

Gary thought for a moment before he began. *He wasn't going to instruct the two operatives on some of the mechanics of centrifuging, in order to show some of the procedures used to create nuclear warheads,* But they already knew a good part of the differences between quantum and digital computing, notwithstanding their knowledge on Nano technology. Also, they both had a good grounding on drones and robotics. *Might as well go on with it.* Gary thought.

"To begin with, there are many different kinds of centrifuges that uses their technologies to separate and enhance the specimens they're working on. There's medical ones, biological ones, and even ones for food, which are my favorite. You know, people who work with advanced Kitchen Aid mixers are actually using rudimentary centrifuges. You can kneed, mix, minimize, maximize, transfer, change, and enhance the flavors of food. But we are not after that, are we? No, we are after atomic isotopes that if centrifuges work as they were designed can, in the end, make very powerful atomic bombs. Just like making a cake."

"What about fusion bombs?" Slade asked.

"Well, Slade, funny that you asked," the little guy was in wonderment at the curiosity of these two hard-bitten soldiers.

"Here is a sentence or two on thermonuclear bombs. We may have a more thorough discussion on it later. These are fusion based instead of fission based like atomic bombs. They are in a different category and much more dangerous than fission initiated atomic bombs. I believe there are only the big five that belong to the thermonuclear club for fusion bombs over 50 Kilotons. They are Russia, China, France, England, and ourselves. We believe India will join the club within the next few years. Now, where was I? Oh yes, back to fission bombs. Okay, the old Stuxnet virus interrupted the spin and harmonics of the centrifuges deep down in Iran's facilities. Some of these centrifuges were totally stopped.

The software written for this was still not sophisticated enough to confuse and possibly place blame on their own nuclear scientist without a wiff coming from the outside. Of course this indicated some of their scientists were screwing up and heads started to roll. Just like Russian philosophy they delve in secrecy. Their centrifuges along with most of their machinery was hidden from the outside world including the International Atomic Energy Agency (IAEA). The IAEA for numerous years were trying to investigate their progress, but Iran lied to them, time and time again, that all of their equipment was pretty much on the surface. The IAEA searched around and only found some storage facilities that held outdate machinery and old centrifuges. What kind of idiots do they think we were!" Gary exclaimed. "It's ironic that they wouldn't let the IAEA inspect their nuclear operation. They might have helped them to untangle the mystery of their failed operation and saved them years of moving forward. They also could've directed them on a wild goose chase. We'll never know. One thing I do know in all my years of my experience is that closed countries like North Korea, China, Russia, and Iran are doing a disservice to the advancement of their technology and their people. All and all the nations with the most advanced technology enjoy the gifts of a better life." Gary now asked, "okay, are we ready to look at the technology that makes fission bombs–the technology behind centrifuges that makes this so important."

Jake and Slade looked at each other shrugged then nodded their heads.

NINETEEN

What kind of Nuclear Bombs?

"**A**s you know, there are two distinct types of nuclear bombs. One is created by a fusion chain reaction and is loosely known as a Thermonuclear bomb. It is based on the Sun's technology. The other is created from fission material which interacts between different isotopes and is called an Atomic Bomb. There are two different Atomic bombs that were used by the United States against Japan to shorten the war in the Pacific Theater. The bomb used against Hiroshima was called **Little boy.** For Nagasaki a bomb call **Fatboy** was used.

These two bombs were atomic but their technology was different. Little Boy was based on using U238 and U235. The driving force for the bomb was behind U235. However, this element is extremely rare in nature to the exact specification of .0007. On the other had U238 is abundant in nature."

"You're not saying that you can change U238 to U235 by using centrifuges?" Jake asked.

Gary thought for a long moment before answering. *He was only going to give them a very light summary of the subject because he knew they were not prepared for a full explanation, most people aren't. You have to have a good background (preparation) leading to the subject. Besides, they didn't have the time. At best it would take months, if not years, before the soldiers were well grounded in the technology.*

"Now, let me finish," Gary implored with a sour look on his face. "No, you cannot change U238 directly to U235 by centrifuges. However, you can increase the proportion of U35 in a sample of uranium which contains U238 and U235 by using centrifuges to separate the isotopes due to their slight mass difference 'effectively enriching' with U235 while removing more U238: this process is called uranium enrichment."

Slade looked at Gary and thought for a long moment before asking, " How long does the process takes, and do you use anything else in the procedure?"

'You're asking the right question." Gary took off his glasses and cleaned and polished them before putting them on. He was a little guy balding with white hair, and a narrow face. But look out for his big brown eyes. They were deep, intense and quick. Just looking at the man exuded intelligence. "Now where was I oh yes, Slade, let's address isotope separation first. Why? Because that's what happens in the centrifuges, to make U235 separate from U238. As the centrifuge is spinning let's say at a rate 50,000 to 70,000 rpm or so we inject a gas like uranium hexafluoride UF6 at a very low temperature causing the heavier U238 isotope to move towards the outer edges of the centrifuge, while the lighter U235 isotope concentrates at the center of the centrifuge."

"But what causes the actual separation? There must be some kind of catalyst besides the gas?" Jake implied with a skeptical look on his face.

Slade took his turn at skepticism. "I've heard about flash points. What triggers a flashpoint and what kind of materials are used?"

"Slow down guys, give me a chance. We'll get to all this shortly." *Gary thought about what he would say next—organizing his subject.*

"Even though U235 and U238 are chemically identical, they have a small mass difference, which allows for separation using a centrifuge. To have any notable progress for this process to move along in order to achieve any significant enrichment, a series of centrifuges are connected together where the slightly enriched uranium from one centrifuge is fed into the next, thus further concentrating the U235. This is called the Cascadian effect. Moreover, to do this in a reasonable fashion, and achieve suitable results before you die you have to connect 20 plus thousand centrifuges together. It's similar to connecting thousands of digital nodes together to greatly increase your computing speed. Except there is no Cascade effect. Each digital node is working on its own segment of the problem while other nodes are working on their segments."

Jake's deep blue eyes were in serious concentration mode before he asked, "what is the difference in mass between the two? You said the weight of their mass was slightly different. Also, what is the percentage rate of U235 to make nuclear weapons?"

"There is a 1.27% difference and this causes the heavier U238 to move toward the walls of the centrifuge. Incidentally, the tails of U235, which is the ends of the U235 enrichment streams are called depleted uranium and are used in ammunition. And to answer your last question, you have to enrich U235 to at least 90 percent to make a viable nuclear weapon."

Slade was at it again. " What makes U238 heavier than U235?"

"Okay that's a good question. You have to remember where doing all of this at the atomic (molecular level). The nucleus of the U-235 atom contains 92 protons and 143 neutrons, giving it an atomic mass of 235 units. The U-238 nucleus also has 92 protons but has 146 neutrons – three more than U-235 – and therefore has a mass of 238 units.

"But what starts a chain reaction?" Jake asked.

"Boy, you guys want to know everything," Gary said, with a twinkle in his deep brown eyes. "Okay let's go another round, and remember let's keep this simple." A chain reaction is initiated when a quantity of fissionable material such as U235 reaches critical mass. And critical mass means when there is a minimum amount of fissile material needed to sustain a self-sustaining chain reaction. Going on, it's the smallest quantity of material required to initiate a continuous fission process where each fission event produces enough neutrons to trigger further fissions in neighboring atoms. Guys, I think we've beat this subject enough to understand that centrifuges are a critical part in making Atomic bombs."

TWENTY

Thumb Number Three

O kay, fellas, let's look behind door number three. Hey guys why don't you take a break while I study this."

"Thanks, boss, they mumbled still thinking about fission bombs."

As Gary moved through the code he could tell not only by the time stamp, but also the logic showed some advancement from the other two thumb drives. It showed improvements on critical pathways that allowed them to untangle their entanglements to neighboring atoms at a faster, cleaner and more direct route. As said before, he could see that they used electromagnetism, like us, to control the bounce of the molecules in order to line them up in a straight line for accurate execution. He knew there was another method called absolute zero. You needed to slow the environment of molecular interaction between the atoms to near Kelvin zero in order to systematically line up the molecules for quantum computation. Again, Gary could see why they were behind the United States. They simply didn't trust their people and scientist enough to allow them to code for them in an open environment. He knew that a good portion of their society didn't trust their government and suspected some of their scientist harbored ill will against the technology.

TWENTY-ONE

Russian Authorities

Reports were coming in that three people came running out of one of the Science and Technology buildings near the lake and they jumped into an old Mercedes Benz sedan, sped away, and then crashed through a barricaded front entrance at the Moscow State University. The nearest police agency or station about a mile away received these reports–Major General Samuil Barinov received the report and he wondered what the heck was going on. They never had any trouble like this before in the campus. First of all, why was the entrance barricaded and why did a chase ensue? That's all he knew, but he also knew that there was much more to this. He called security at MSU and for some reason, they wouldn't or couldn't provide any more information than what he already had. He could smell something amiss, so he kicked it upstairs to Lieutenant Colonel Nikita Grankin.

He went to Nikita's office and knocked. "Come in, yes Samuil what is it? You can take a chair." After getting somewhat comfortable he began, "sir, I just received a call from MSU security that there was an incident on their campus a while ago. Apparently, there were three people that ran out of one of the Science and Technology buildings and jumped into an old Mercedes Benz and sped away. Also, a barricade was set up in time at the front entrance to stop the intruders. That old tank of a car just busted through and turned left and headed up the thoroughfare. One of the security cars gave chase, but couldn't keep up with the Benz and eventually lost them in a neighborhood near the campus."

"Did they get the plates?" "Yes they did and we are running them now." "That's good work, Samuil. At least we may have a start. Oh, was there any another cars in the parking lot?" "Yes, there was a fairly new Lada parked close to the Benz, and we're also running those plates. Good job Samuil. As he left, Nikita thought about all of this and wondered if either or both cars were stolen. He guess *he would find out.*

TWENTY-TWO

New Digs

After the two Delta Force ops gathered back into the room with Gary, they called Ernie back in. While Jake was on the sat phone with encryption in place, Slade instructed the other two to thoroughly clean the place and look for anything out of the ordinary like listening devices. The old place they just left was cleansed to the nines–nothing there to find. The old place may lay fallow for weeks or even months before it is used again.

When the connection was terminated with his boss, Jim Radke, he told the crew there would be a discussion with the powers to be if they should go now or wait a day or two. In that case they might as well relax and have a bite to eat while waiting for the phone call.

"What will happen?" Ernie ventured. Ernesto was a bachelor like Jake and had been with the agency for five years. He was young, but seem to have the look and experience of an older person. In addition, he was an excellent wheel man–the guy could drive. He was the quiet type and always focused on his orders. He liked his job and one day hoped he could be head of logistics like Steve Olson.

"Okay, who's cooking? Jake said with his crooked smile. Everyone looked at him as if he was Wolfgang Puck. Slade, for sure, knew his culinary skills were legendary. After all, he always had five lovelies at his beck and call to match his five muscle cars. And they all loved his cooking besides his other delights. Even though Slade had two gorgeous and very bright daughters, he was still a little jealous of his buddy. He remembered back how they met, it was at an agency poker game with a group of Delta Force ops playing weekly. Jake was new to the agency and was invited to play with the dangerous four. The hours rolled by until Slade and Jake were the only ones left. If he recalled correctly, Jake won with a straight flush to his full boat. Afterward they stood up eye-to-eye and Slade saluted and said welcome to the brotherhood. Even though they didn't know each other well at that point, they became great friends, and watched each other's back from there on in.

Jake looked in to the fridge and saw a nice plump chicken ready to go with two large bottles of Caesar dressing and a large container of sour cream among other items.. Next he rummaged around the drawers and found a large casserole dish. "Hey, Ernie, do we have a spice drawer?"

"What's a blasted spice drawer? Never heard of any such thing."

Jake chuckled and ask if there were any spices.

"Beats me, buddy. I've only been here a couple days. The agency moved me from another safe house to here. And to be honest, I didn't know why until I got the call to save your butts."

"Okay, I'll look around." Jake found a spice carousel loaded with spices. He looked in the lower bin of the fridge and found a package of parmesan cheese. He turned around to the other three and said, " how about Caesar chicken." Everyone cheered!

Slade stepped up to the kitchen counter to help his old friend. "What are our chances of being moved tonight?"

"I hope not because I'm into making a great creamy Caesar chicken for us. You know how I love to cook." Just as Jake was ready to serve dinner with scallop potatoes and baby carrots on the side, they heard a car pull up next to the curb.

TWENTY-THREE

Changing Events

Jake and Slade rushed to a window in another room to get a better look at the car and the surrounding area, and it also gave them better cover. Two men got out of the auto wearing black suits, ties and Fedora hats. They stop, looked around and nodded to a third person in the sedan.

"What do you think, Jake?" Slade asked with a serious look on his scruffy face.

"They're not Russians because, first of all, they couldn't find us this quickly. Also, they're dressed like Americans."

"I wonder why they're seeing us?" Slade asked.

"I don't know, but I think they're CIA or NIA. Look, one of them is showing a badge with his pen light on it. Looks like CIA. Let's move to the front door, but let's be extremely cautious," Jake said with a serious look, his blue eyes narrowing on his face.

As they approached the front door, Slade motioned Gary and Ernie toward the back of the house just in case. When the doorbell chimed, Jake opened the door cautiously while Slade hung back. An arm came through showing a CIA badge and a voice followed. "I'm Thomas Eden and my partner is Clyde Simpson and we're CIA."

Jake let them in, checked their credentials and after introductions, led both gentlemen to a couch in the living room. "What about the guy in the backseat?" Jake inquired. "Oh, he's posting in case we need him." Clyde said.

"I'll have you know you have interrupted a great creamy Caesar chicken dinner we were about to enjoy. Would you and Clyde join us this evening? I hate to see the meal go cold and not eaten. I think there is enough for all us."

Slade got Gary and Ernie from one of the bedrooms and after they were introduced, everyone sat down at the big round table while Slade got two more table settings and Jake placed two large casserole dishes in the center of the table. He looked rather stylish wearing a kitchen apron that barely fit him. He then asked about the lone wolf in the car? Clyde looked at Tom before he spoke. "He's okay–that's his job."

"Can we bring him some leftovers?" Slade inquired.

"You sure can and plus it would give you a chance to meet him." Tom said scratching his curly blond hair.

Slade shot Jade a quick look after the last exchange, and Jake nodded.

"We're all having soft drinks and coffee. What would you and Tom like?"

"Coffee is fine for us," Clyde replied.

"Okay, what's going on?" Jake queried while eating a mouthful of scalloped potatoes.

"Well, first of all, Romania, which is a NATO member, will be holding elections soon and one of their candidates that holds 23% of the popular vote believes in communism and is leaning too far to the right as Putin does. He even emulates Putin, like riding a horse bare chested and fishing like Putin does. Quite frankly, we are a little worried about him." Tom said as he asked to pass the dinner rolls around.

"Are any of the other NATO members show leaning in this direction?" Jake asked as he took a sip of his Pepsi.

"We've been researching this and so far we haven't found any evidence of this. With Finland and Sweden recently joining NATO, I think NATO will stay intact without any negative changes occurring." Tom conjectured.

"Ya I think will be okay." Clyde said as he joined the conversation. "But we have trouble brewing in the wind. With the Biden administration giving the nod to Ukraine using US made long range ATACMS missiles this will surely increase tensions between the two countries and possibly steer Putin's thinking about using strategic nuclear weapons against

Ukraine. Hell, Ukraine has already fired a number of these missiles and hit civilian and military airfields in the Kursk region of Russia. They've also fired more of these missiles to other regions. Russia now avows to retaliate and if this keeps on, the war will escalate to the point that Putin will use nuclear weapons. Then what will happen?"

"The Atomic Clock will finally strike twelve and world war III will likely happen." Jake conjectured. I hope the administration has this well in hand and is doing everything possible to stave this off. Here we thought the conflict between Iran and Israel was dangerous who are we kidding ourselves."

"But what are we actually doing about it?" Slade said while asking for more of that delicious Caesar chicken. "I mean with that lame duck President doing nothing and just waiting for his term to end. I feel like we are sitting ducks for something terrible to happen. Thank God, the President elect isn't waiting. His transition team is already well under way and he is strategizing how he can manage Putin. He also will have the border closed soon after entering office. Further he will introduce the most powerful taxing and regulatory package that we have seen in decades. Mexico and Canada are already talking to him as our other countries. The President of Mexico has already shut down their southern border. This is happening now not on January 20th. President Biden could only dream of such things."

"Okay Tom, this brings us full circle as to why you and Clyde are here?" Jake said. While Ernie and Gary cleaned off the table and hand cleaned the dirty dishes the four agents continued their conversation.

TWENTY-FOUR

Now, What?

"The Pentagon has sent us here because of what's happening in Ukraine. The war now has really spiked since North Korea has been sending troops and equipment to Russia to engage the Ukrainians. And as I said the Ukrainians are using US made ATACMS missiles and are firing them in to the Kursk region of Russia. And right now the United States isn't doing much with very little diplomatic talks with their counter parts."

Tom took a moment to gather his thoughts before continuing. "These missiles are really quite deadly since they are hard to take down because of their flight path. They fly like regular ballistics until they get near their target and then their flight path changes to a 90 degree angle. It's like they go around a corner in the sky when they zero in on their targets. They can be carried and fired from a two wheel cart or from a battery. They presently contain two different types of warheads. The first is a cluster configuration of bomblets that activates the explosions in multiple layers in a wide area. Of course after the war they will pose a danger to the civilian population in unexploded bomblets. The other type is a single warhead designed to take out hardened facilities. The original version developed and manufactured by Lockheed Martin has a range of about 200 miles. However the Army is developing a slimmer version of this type of missile that has a range of 500 miles. This could possibly put Moscow within that range. If the United States allows this, and it is a distinct possibility with the Biden Administration. Putin for sure will use tactical nukes against Ukraine. So having said that here are your new orders." Clyde handed the two black ops a large Manila envelope.

"What about are previous orders?" Jake questioned.

"They've been cancelled and reclassified as of now," Tom said.

Slade jumped into the conversation and asked, "Will there be follow up to the original plan? I mean, the Middle East is still in a dangerous situation, with or without are help."

"Don't know about that guys, we only follow orders like you. Everything is highly compartmentalized." Clyde said. "Oh, by the way, if you don't mind, we will be staying here tonight. I know there's plenty of space, and we'll be leaving first thing in the morning."

" Now, let's close up shop and enjoy the rest of the evening." Jake said with his crooked smile.

"But what about Zeke in the car, will he be alright?" Slade asked, looking at Jake.

Clyde looking at the two black op responded, "Don't worry, that's his job–covering our backs."

TWENTY-FIVE

Russian Authority Progress

Nikita got the old Benz license report back and found that the car belonged to one of the professors at MSU. They brought the professor, Dr. Maxim Lenin, in for questioning even though he filed a stolen vehicle report. He was at a loss as much as they were. What about the Lada he asked. The vehicle disappeared along with the paper work. At this point it's as good as being lost. However, the important fact that was uncovered was that Dr. Lenin was a team member working on Quantum Mechanics and Computing. With this, all kinds of flags were going up in Nikita's mind. He knew this could really be important. A dragnet was already thrown around the area of the campus and it yield nothing. *They would have to expand the area and work grid by grid,* he thought. Nikita knew there was much more to this then what meets the eye. For crying out loud, three people come running out of the Science and Technology building. He knew some of the personnel that worked in these buildings were researching Quantum science. Security said they spotted them on the second floor before they blew past the security desk located on the first floor. They even questioned the security person on duty when the intruders checked in. She said their id credentials looked

authentic. The little guy with the glasses did most of the talking in Russian. The other two spoke a little Russian too. They were big with athletic builds and reminded her of the old KJB. The building security team then asked her why they reminded her of the KJB. She told them they were very casual not tight at all, but they were routinely looking around as if something were coming. When asked why they were here, the little guy spoke up and said they were here to see an associate. She asked for the associate's name, checked the list and made a call. A male voice answered and said he was in the restroom, and the voice on the other end wanted to know if she wanted to wait. She looked at the three in front of her with impatience and said no. She then patted down all three and found nothing. The three said good day and walked to the nearest bank of elevators. She did say one of the big guys looked back at her and smiled. He could tell that she was mildly attracted to him.

Nikita asked the building's security if there was anything else and they didn't know or they wouldn't tell him. He would wait another day to see if anything else would developed. If there wasn't any more progress, he would have no choice but to contact the Federal Security Service (FSB) and give them all the information he had. He hoped he wouldn't get a butt chewing for waiting an extra day. He would check with Samuil tomorrow to see if he knew of anything else before kicking it upstairs.

TWENTY-SIX

Zoey

After Tom and Clyde had coffee and left early the next morning. Slade and Gary sat around the big round table nourishing their coffee while Jake cooked breakfast. He told them that they would get to the documents after they ate.

"Good idea," Gary said. While Jake was cooking, his sat phone ringed and he picked up on the second one.

"Well if it isn't Zip." Jake exclaimed. He motioned Slade to continue cooking breakfast while he talked to his girlfriend, Zoey Chamberlain. He walked to another room. "How long has it been sweets?" Jake said with a wide smile on his face.

"Don't sweets me!" Zoey huffed. You know messenger just goes so far. Do you know it's been almost two months since we have seen each other? You would've thought to at least call me. What were you thinking. You know that really hurts, honey. We've known each other for well over two years and we have been through a lot. I would have expected more, and I bet you don't even know where we first met."

"Now hold on a moment sweetheart." Jake said in a conciliatory tone. "First of all, we first met on a Royal Caribbean cruise ship steaming toward Barbados if I'm not mistaken. You came up behind me in the bar and asked how well I did at the stud poker table? And when I turned I was staring into the most amazing blue eyes that I have ever seen."

"Oh quit, you're already making my legs wobbly, you big galoot."

"No, I can't quit now. I remembered peering at your beautiful face and your magnificent head of dark silverfish hair. I was thinking I better watch out because I could be playing with fire. When you excused yourself to go to the ladies powder room, I turned and watched you go. You had a gorgeous athletic build, and that athletic stride–well I didn't mind playing with fire from then on."

"Oh, Jake, you're such a sailor."

"Just a sailor for you only, my sweets. Anyway, it's great hearing your voice again, and honestly, I've been wanting to call you, but I've been so blasted busy."

"Where are you at, honey?"

"You know I can't tell you that. except to say somewhere in Central Europe."

"Your birthday is coming up soon and I want to give you a special surprise," Zoey said with a twinkle in her blue eyes.

"Don't remind me of my birthday, please." Jake said with chuckle in his voice.

"Oh, come on, don't be a sore loser!...Oh, that reminds me, are you still carrying the zipper I gave you when we first met?" Zoey said wrinkling her nose.

"Sure am, sweets. How could I ever forget what it represents?: Jake said with a hearty laugh. "Hon, I've got to go. The guys are calling me. I promise I'll do better calling you, and I can't wait to get back to see you again."

"You better get back here safe and sound, you hear, sailor?"

"Yes, ma'am!" Jake saluted and said *bye my sweets* and broke the encrypted sat connection. He thought about the wonderful vacation they had at Chesapeake Bay. It was only for a weekend, but they both wanted it to be for a lifetime. God, she was lovely woman, but now back to business. He hurried back to the kitchen to see what was left and of course with Slade around there wasn't much.

Slade looked up from his plate of scrambled eggs and sausage and said with a sly smile, "how's lovey dovey doing?"

Jake just snorted as he got what was left. "Okay guys lets finish up and check out our new orders." He ate what was left from the pans warming on the stove burners wondering what kind of heat they were getting themselves in to.

TWENTY-SEVEN

Orders

After the dishes were cleared in cleaned the three men sat at the big round table. They first read the new orders from the Deputy Secretary of Homeland Security, James Radke. It indicated that members of the Mossad were now armed with the new Stuxnet II virus, and since Russia was lagging far behind the US in quantum technology, they were instructed to secretly insert the deadly worm into Iran's nuclear systems and thus send them back at least another ten years.

After reading the direct orders again, Jake began placing the documents and photographs on the table. They were showing where various missile and tactical weapons installations were set in and around Moscow. The black ops whistled when they saw what they were looking at.

"Look at all these sites." Jake said. "There must be at least twenty of them. How on earth are we going to shut all of them down in a short period of time? Any ideas, Gary?"

Gary studied the installations to see if there were any symmetry to their locations. His idea was he knew Russia had been financially strapped for years and would cut costs wherever they could. As he was inspecting the photographs a kernel of an idea was building in his mind on how to maximize the software and systems destruction of these sites in the shortest amount of time.

"Jake, doesn't the United States have an world-wide schematic that shows all the growing connections on the Internet on a minute-by-minute basis?" Gary ventured.

"I believe we do, but it's top secret (for your eyes only) classification."

"Since I work for the Department of Homeland Security, I believe I can up my security to this level depending on the situation."

"Well wouldn't you think our present situation warrants this? Gary responded.

"I'm surprised that James didn't indicate this in his letter. He is almost always informed on events and situation around the world and how it relates to homeland security. Slade get on the horn and talk to the boss."

" Already on it, chief."

While Jake and Gary were waiting, Gary was explaining the finer points of the world-wide internet connections, and how it relates to their present situation.

"Okay Slade, what did the big kahuna say?"

"He said to hold on. He's going to talk to Mary Stinson and suspects it won't take too long to get her done."

"Slade get over here. Gary is going to give us an explanation on how this all work."

"I'm going to make this quick–just glossing over the important points. The Internet evolved from the Pentagon's Advanced Research Project Agency (ARPA).The forerunner of the Internet was launched in 1969 between UCLA and Scientific Data Systems in Menlo Park and was known as ARPANET. After years of development and testing by various governmental and civilian agencies. it was released to the public in 1995. Fast forward to 2023 and 24 the Internet is now using IPv6 because of its rapid expansion."

"What does IPv6 mean?" Slade asked.

"You would have to ask that? Huh," Gary replied. *Well let's see,* Gary thought. "The Internet started with IPv2 for space, and then it went to IPv4 around 2010 and now it's at IPv6 for expansion purposes."

"But how is that determined?" Slade persisted.

Gary thought how to explain this in laymen terms, and he couldn't find any easy way to do it. So he looked at Slade and began. "The eight groups of IPv6 make a total of 32 hexadecimal digits, four bits each, which makes a total of 128 bits. RFC 4291 says that the preferred representation of an IPv6 address is X:X:X:X:X:X:X:X and RFC 5952 recommends that the address is written in lowercase. In other words, as the internet expanded, it needed more representation to define itself. It was IPv2, then IPv4 and now IPv6 and in the future it will need IPv8."

"Explain hexadecimal representation to me."

"Oh, come on, Slade, let's not get down in the weeds. You guys only need to know it involves expansion. As it is, I went too far and I don't want to continue down this particular path, cause it's really not that important to where we are going."

Just then, Jake's sat phone vibrated and he picked up on the second vibe. He already knew who it was by the photo on the phone.

TWENTY-EIGHT

Secretary, Mary Stinson

Jake put his finger to his lips to signify silence. "Hello, Madam Secretary," Jake replied.

"Do you have your encryption on?" Mary responded.

"Yes, Madam."

"Jake, let's dispense with the formalities."

"Okay, Mary. What do we have?"

"Do you have your orders from James?" Mary asked.

"Yes, we received them last night from the CIA. After they left this morning, we unsealed the top secret red banner and opened the contents of the large Manila envelope."

"Naughty boy! You know you shouldn't open top secret material until you receive an encrypted phone call or an official letter to put you at that level."

"Mary, I'm going to be blunt. I was in the head and Slade was outside checking the car for any low jacks. Gary already apologized about this."

"Good, now I want to tell you how important this is. You know as well as I how dangerous Russia is. Hell, they even have more nuclear warheads then we do. The Bear is armed to the teeth. They even have more tactical nukes then we have."

"I know, Madam Secretary. And I also know we need to tip toe around the Bear when we're snooping. With Putin being paranoid about the Ukrainian war, we don't know what he will do." Jake replied.

"That's why we pulled you guys off the Middle East situation. You did an excellent job finding how advance they were in quantum mechanics. The new thumb drive tests went off without a hitch. Although you narrowly missed being captured."

"Yeah, that was pretty scary." Jake quipped. "I know you and James read the report I sent. Do you know where that 85 Mercedes came from?"

"I do know the police are throwing all their weight on this and the Federal Security Service (FSB) will be contacted soon, especially when they find out, and here goes my secret, the Benz was registered to Dr. Maxim Lenin. The good doctor is part of a team that is working on quantum science."

"Oh, oh," Jake whispered. "I guess we stole the wrong car."

"Da!!" The Secretary exclaimed. "Well, here we thought you saved our bacon with a clean escape. Time will tell, Jake. Enough of the chit chat, we need to get down to disarming Russia's nuclear armament."

"And how are we going to do that?" Jake queried, clenching his left hand.

"Like I said, testing our newest quantum technology at the University of Moscow worked beautifully. We now know where Russia is on the spectrum, and we also believe we now have the means to shut down most if not all of Russia's nuclear capability."

"Wow!" That's all Jake could muster.

"Now listen carefully," Mary said. "Gary will guide you and Slade on how we are going to do this. You may have to travel to some of the locations, but we're not sure yet. The main tool we'll be using was developed by the Army some time ago and is constantly being updated. It's for your eyes only at this time. That's part of the reason why you, Gary and Slade have been reclassified as top secret, and my phone call."

"Did Gary know about this?" Jake asked.

"No. Gary only knew to see if the new thumb drives worked as designed, and they do."

"If we're successful, and Lord knows we better be, I suppose that China will be the preeminent power besides us."

"You're correct, Jake." Mary answered. "On another note, you're making it a little more difficult for us."

Jake searched his mind trying to find a reason why madam Secretary would say that. "What happened madam?"

"You still don't know do you?" Mary quipped.

"No I don't. I only hope it wasn't a monumental blunder."

Mary thought for a minute on the other end. "Jake, we just went through part of this." Mary huffed. "The car you stole belonged to Dr. Maxim Lenin, and he is a team member and a researcher on Quantum

Mechanics as I have indicated. But he isn't just any old researcher, he is Russia's premier Quantum Scientist."

"Oh God!" Jake exclaimed. "They're going to throw the Federal Security Service (FSB) on us. That's akin to the KGB. Will we be alright?" Jake asked.

Mary thumbed the back of her smart phone before inserting. "You didn't know, and the Lada would have never made it."

"I know but the heat will really be on us now."

"You'll be okay as long as you follow our plan to the letter." Mary responded.

"Well I'm still worried about the Bear, madam. Won't they lash out to another nation, perhaps us. I mean I would be pissed if someone shut down our nuclear capability."

" I hear ya, but our technology and actions will confuse Russia to such an extent they won't know what to do. To them it will be like magic." Mary thought for a moment. " We're hoping cooler heads at the Kremlin will prevail and stop Putin from making any rash decisions. Besides, if we knock off enough of their firepower they would think twice about attacking anyone. And we have a another secret."

Jake thought for a long moment, "what's that?" He asked.

"All in due time, Mr. Cannon, all in due time." Mary said with a sly voice.

"Well in that case what is the tool will be using?" Jake asked.

"Gary will fill you guys in. Now get crackin'" The connection went dead.

TWENTY-NINE

Federal Security Service (FSB)

Agent Damien Petrov was the first to receive the official report from Lieutenant Colonel, Nikita Grantin from the Police Agency. The FSB basically followed, in the same footsteps and structure of the American FBI. Like the American FBI he was the agent in charge for the sector around the MSU campus. What he read was very troubling and could have national implications to the security of his country. He had to read it twice for it to hit home like a sledge hammer. He quickly called an official meeting with his best agents to form their strategy based on the information he had received so far and assign them around Moscow to find these people. He didn't know who they were, but he needed to confine them for questioning as soon as possible. Like Nikita said the car they stole belonged to one of the foremost Quantum scientist in Russia. So far, there was a dead end on the Lada. The credentials used to rent the car were bogus, but Damien suspected the three people they were looking for were the ones that rented the Lada.

"Sir, yes Ivan. How come this is so important?"

"We don't know yet, but they may have gotten away with top secret information on our Quantum Science. You should know that Quantum Mechanics and AI are on the top of our list for research. We cannot let the West get ahead of us in this area. Now we need to report this to Vladimir Putin and he is not going to be happy about this. In fact, knowing his temper, he may make an example out of a few of us."

"God, I hope it's not any of us," Denis Babkin said, with terror written across his chubby face.

"No, no, we are too important to him for us to be fodder. If it happens it will be some poor old smoe. Although, undoubtedly it will be made public to strike fear into the general populace. Now does anyone have any evidence on what is going on?" Damien asked with a stern look on his face. No one spoke. "Okay, the police agencies are already searching a wide area around the MSU campus, grid by grid. Let's hit the ground and help our brethren. The more we are, comrades, and the harder we search the sooner something may turn up–get going!"

As Damien watch his troops exit the conference room not saying a word, he couldn't help to think that something very ominous was going to happen. He knew it was probably early in the investigation and he probably was making a mountain out of a mole hill, but dammit he hardly ever had this feeling before as he began to pace.

THIRTY

The Big Round Table

As Jake was walking back to the big round table, he was running different scenarios in his head on how the United States was going to pull this off. He assumed that this wasn't going to be easy, otherwise they wouldn't be here. He was beginning to get a handle on some of this. To him, the big picture basically looked like a two-step plan. First, do a real test using the three Quantum thumb drives on the University of Moscow. You can run all the simulated tests back home, but it's not the same thing. He knew the US wouldn't be spending this kind of money on Quantum technology and Artificial Intelligence unless there was a huge payoff.

"Okay, what did Mary say to you?" Slade asked.

"Well, let's see." Jake said while tapping his fingers on the table.

"Come on, Jake!" Slade huffed. "Don't you be coy with me. I know sometin' is up or she wouldn't be calling us."

"Okay, fellas. I already know you know a lot about this." Jake looked at Gary and grinned.

Slade looked at his friends and said, "you guys keeping secrets from me–huh?"

"Ya, I was wondering if you still wanted to buy my 67 Nova?"

"Oh, cut the crap, Jake. I know you better than that!" Slade exclaimed.

"Alright, Gary you have the floor. Poor Slade here is about to go nuts"

"Okay, I gather I pretty much know what you and Madam Secretary were talking about." Gary took a long moment to collect his thoughts and continued. "As we know," while looking at Slade, "the break in at MSU and the insertion of the three thumb drives was a sure-fire test to see if the Quantum drives worked properly, plus it gave us Russia's current stance on Quantum technology. And I also went through the papers in the car we stole to see if there was any significance, and there was. For one, we just happened to steal the auto that belonged to Maxim Lenin. I know you guys don't know who he is, but I do. He is one of Russia's foremost scientist on Quantum Mechanics and Computing and AI. So now we have to be doubly cautious, if we weren't already." Both black ops nodded their heads.

"Why didn't you tell us this before?" Jake questioned.

"It must have slipped my mind. You know I have a lot to gather and disseminate to you fellows and apologize for the slippage."

"Please don't let this happen again. It could mean the difference between life or death." Slade said, with concern written across his face.

Gary thought for a moment before answering, "I will fellas, I guess it was just a moment of carelessness. Now getting back to the main subject, if their Quantum technology was up to snuff with ours, we would've headed to the Middle East ourselves and gave the gift of giving and giving, and giving … to Iran instead of handing it off to the Mossad. So now we have bigger fish to fry–much bigger."

"What is this about?" Slade said as a frown appeared above his steely black eyes."

"Well, Slade, since the test at MSU went perfectly and we found that the Bear is quite a bit behind us on quantum mechanics, we will attempt to shut down most if not all of Russia's nuclear capability."

Slade let out a low whistle. "How can this be?" Slade questioned.

"Let me collect something and I'll be right back"

"How are we going to this, Jake" Slade pleaded with his eyes.

"Let Gary explain this to us. I'm sure it will be interesting." This was the second thing he was looking for. Jake thought.

THIRTY-ONE

The Screens

Gary brought out two laptops and placed them side-by-side on the big round table and faced them toward Jake and Slade. On one he pulled up running text, while on the other the screen seemed to expand with small widgets everywhere.

"What are all those tiny ridges?" Slade asked.

"Just a minute while I increase the size of the map." Gary said.

"A map!" Both soldiers exclaimed. "What are those tiny icons on the screen?" Jake asked, scratching his nose.

"Well guys, they are the standard icons that represent electronic pieces on the screen. I'll zoom in closer. You already know most of the figures. Right?" Gary asked.

"Look as the servers, mirrored servers, routers, switches, lines, flags, IP, and IPSs grow.

"Is this in real time?" Slade questioned.

"Sure is, and some of them are rotating depending on the time they need."

"You mean the addresses?" Slade ventured.

"Ya, some are static, the others dynamic." Gary volunteered. "The static ones are usually for larger businesses and companies. They usually need the Internet Provider Service on all the time. The rotating (dynamic) addresses are for houses etc. When one is done it switches off and gives the same address to another house etc. This is done to save space."

"What about the other screen?" Slade inquired.

"That's the code aided by AI, writing all the activity on the growing map."

"So you're telling us as each connection is made through an IPS, the address is recorded along with its electronic signature it requires to fulfill its purpose for servers, routers, switches flags etc."

"That's correct, Jake. The technology is truly amazing. It also identifies, in real time, any botnets that are forming. It also recognizes when any section of the net goes dark, as in dark net."

"Oh my God!" Slade exclaimed. "How long has this been in place?"

"The Army developed this technology around 2010."

"You're telling us the Pentagon knows, in real time, what is going on in the world electronically." Jake said. "And look, the world is underlaid below all the e-signatures on the map and the boundaries and countries can dynamically change. Incredible, just incredible!" Jake exclaimed, showing excitement in his voice. "So I gather this technology will help us shut down Russia's nuclear capability. Am I right?"

"You sure are Jake," Gary said.

"But how?" Slade asked, his dark eyes under intense concentration.

THIRTY-TWO

Land Based Nuclear Installations

"We still haven't tested this new technology remotely. So let's try it." Gary thought for a moment on how he was going to approach this. "Slade, pick a spot on the map." Gary instructed.

"What do you mean?" Slade asked with a blank face.

"Just pick an IPS anywhere on the map."

Slade reach to the Northeast section of Russia, in the Siberian region, and pointed to an IPS.

Gary added another screen and entered the IP address and after a few seconds viola! A picture of a building with its name, address and general location showing other features within a thousand meters perimeter appeared on the screen. The two soldiers were shocked, to say the least, to see all of this information on the screen from a few keystrokes. It was somewhat similar to Google Earth, but more detailed and identified by an IP address instead of a physical address.

"How did you do this" Slade asked.

"Well the technology has been around for years, but we expanded on it with the help of AI. It even shows what kind of technology the structures are using, if any."

Slade asked again. "What do you mean?"

"We can tell if quantum or digital or a combination of both are being used. We can also tell if analog technology is in use or really nothing at all. In this case, we're looking at Novosibirsk State University. Their main research are in quantum optics, photonics, and related areas within quantum science. Of course, they are using quantum mechanics to uncover these secrets. Yuri even studied there for a time."

"Oh, I almost forgot. There is another piece. The Army invented a technology that allows soldiers to see through normal physical object such as building facades and walls.

This has been in the Army's purview for years. It helps the arm forces greatly reduce the costs of losing lives. It's loosely based on x-ray technology.

"This is twilight stuff." Jake opinioned. "So how is this all going to work?"

"First, we enter the IP address of the target we want to investigate. Next, AI shows us the interior of the structure, and I mean everything including bathrooms. And before you ask, it also shows people moving within the structure and in some cases who some of those people are."

"Holy smokes!" Slade declared. "Now I know why this is so valuable to our armed forces. Before this, we had to rely on Nano technology to develop insects and bees to fly around and in and out of structures taking pictures of what was going on and relaying that information to the commanding officer's (CO) hand held computer. And based on the photographs and information it told the CO, it helped decide go/no go for the troops. It was excellent technology for recognizance, but lacked real time optics."

"You're exactly right, Slade. Now we have all the tools working together in harmony to do the unthinkable: take down a country without exploding a single bomb, and at the same time render them toothless. However, there are a few twists and turns we need to do before we can do the unthinkable. Unfortunately, Mother Russia hasn't fully digitized a few of their land based nuclear installations and that's where you guys come in."

The two intel ops looked at each other and nodded their heads. "I know there was currency, and that's why Jake and I had to be here, but we thought it was just for MSU." Slade said, rubbing his broad chin.

Gary stepped in, "Ya, the orders have changed along with being re-classified and now it looks like the three of us will be going on a sightseeing tour. After all, like our visas states, we are tourist."

"The question is we only have 24 days left on our visas, and will it be enough?" Jake replied.

"Time will tell." Gary answered. "Okay, the software has already identified the land based nuclear installations that are either manual or analog, and thank God there are only a couple of them. The screen shows them coming from the east to the west. So I think we should start at the east end and then go west, young man, go west. What'll think guys?" Gary asked.

Jake studied the terrain around each identified land based nuclear installation, for natural cover before replying. "Based on limited information I have from a strategic point of view, I think we should start here."

"Funny that you should say that, because I believe Madam Secretary would have said the same thing." Gary replied.

Jake just snorted and continued peering at the screen.

THIRTY-THREE

Land Based Nuclear Missiles

Gary thought for a long moment before he tackled the next subject. "Okay guys what I am about to tell you, as they say, is for your eyes only. So let's look at the current crop of land based nuclear war heads that the big five have. They are very scary and on an emotional level I can only say, 'God help us'."

"The terrifying true scale of nuclear weapons is beyond what most people can imagine. The nuclear weapons of today are far more powerful than the two used in WW II. As an example, the B83 nuclear bomb, the largest in the Russia's arsenal, is 2,000 times more powerful than the bomb dropped on Hiroshima. This single nuclear bomb could destroy an entire city like Beijing causing millions of death and injuries, not to mention the infrastructure of the city."

"Good God, where are we going with this!" Slade exclaimed with terror creeping into his gravelly voice.

"Just a minute Slade, let me finish this. The information is paramount describing the scale we are looking at."

"China's Dongfeng 5 missile is another example of the terrifying power of nuclear weapons. It can carry up to 12 warheads using MIRV technology."

"What does that exactly mean?" Slade asked, continuing with his questions.

"It means a Multiple Independently Targetable Reentry Vehicle (MIRV) is a nuclear warhead that can be released from a missile to hit multiple targets. In the cold war era these types of warheads were mainly confined to Intercontinental Ballistic Missiles (ICBMs). Never mind the vehicle they can be carried on, nowadays, because each bomblet itself can have incredible power. Furthermore, in this age, they have their own engines and GPS systems for control guidance."

"In regards to China's Dongfend 5 missile, each of their 12 warheads are 66 times more powerful than the Hiroshima bomb. If aimed at a city like Washington, D.C., the impact would be catastrophic with over a million fatalities and three million injuries including third degree radiation burns.

Russia's R-36 missile known as the "Satan" missile can carry multiple nuclear weapons with immense destructive power. Some versions can deliver a single warhead up to 20 megatons, which is over1,300 times as powerful as the Hiroshima bomb.

And it doesn't stop there!" Gary blurted. "At the top of the list is Mother Russia's RS-28 Sarmat missile, nicknamed "Satan 2." This monster can carry up to 15 warheads and potentially deliver a 50 megaton bomb, causing unimaginable destruction to cities like New York, Chicago and Los Angeles.

Even though some countries may face setbacks and even scale back some of these terrible nuclear weapons it doesn't mean we are safe. It still means that even a few could cause unimaginable damage. The true scale of modern nuclear weapons shows that in a nuclear war, there are no winners–only devastating loss for humanity. And this is only for land based nuclear installations."

"That's right." Jake said. "This doesn't cover sea-going nuclear technology.

THIRTY-FOUR

Sea Going Nuclear Submarine Technology I

Gary walked back to the big round table and sat down again, and formed his thoughts. "The United States mainly has 18 Ohio class submarines of which 14 are Trident II nuclear ballistic missile submarines. It can carry up to 24 nuclear missiles with 8 MIRV warheads apiece which are 30 times more powerful than the Hiroshima bomb. A single Trident II can devastate a city like Moscow, resulting in 2.8 million immediate deaths with nearly 5 million injuries most from third degree radiation burns.

Now let's look at Russia's side of the equation. They have 16 nuclear-powered ballistic missile submarines(SSBNs) that are considered a key part of its strategic deterrent. The Russian Navy has one of the world's largest submarine fleets with an estimated 64 vessels in total."

"What are some of their subs and their capabilities?" Slade asked, amazed at all the deaths that Gary was inferring.

"I was just getting to that. The Borie-class is about 560 ft. long and 43 ft. in diameter, and can travel at speeds of up to 29 mph underwater. They are smaller than the Typhoon class but can carry more missiles due to the lighter Bulava SLBM (Sea Launched Ballistic Missile).

Now the next class of nuclear ballistic submarines is the Typhoon class. These submarines were developed under Project 941 and were designed to match the SLBM armament of Ohio-class submarines. The 941 project was the Soviet Akula class (Akyna) meaning shark. They were bigger than the Borie-class with plenty of fire power, and were very fast with speeds up to 38 knots.

Another class was the Akula-II. These nuclear-powered attack submarines specialized in intelligence gathering, anti-submarine warfare, and anti-surface warfare.

The P-8 Poseidon sub used by several countries can track Russian submarine activities. One of the United States based submarine farms is based in Keflavik near Reykjavik, Iceland."

"Your answers lead us to more and more questions my friend." Slade said. "Who are you really. After all, we have been working closely together on this mission, and as you know it is very dangerous. Now are orders are changed and it looks like we will be in Mother Russia for some time, and I hope what we are doing will be within the time frames of our visas.

THIRTY-FIVE

Gary's Story

"**W**ell, I suppose you want to know more about me than what my dossier says. After all, you have that right since your United States has borrowed me from my Homeland. Right now, to reiterate, we are working on a very dangerous assignment side-by-side and you have a right to know who I am."

"Gary, I'd say that's about right." Jake said as he studied the Israeli nuclear scientist intently.

"Well, as you know, I was born and raised in the city of Haifa, which forms part of the Haifa metropolitan area, the third most populous metropolitan area in Israel. It is home to the Bahá'í Faith's Bahá'í World Centre and is a UNESCO World Heritage Site and a destination for Bahá'í pilgrimage. I studied there until I was 18. By then, I had already learned four languages and was a mathematics prodigy at an early age. I got married soon after I turned twenty and have one beautiful daughter and hopefully she won't be doing what I'm doing."

"What's her name?" Jake asked.

"It's Aliza and my wife's name is Sarah."

"What does Aliza mean in your language?" Jake continued.

"In Hebrew it means "Joyful", and she is simply a beautiful child and Sarah is already making plans for her Batmizvah. The event is usually held just after a girl's 12th birthday."

"Well congratulations to you and Sarah," both soldiers beamed.

"I bet she's as smart as Papa. Am I right?' Slade questioned.

"Well let's put it this way," Gary responded. "she is already beating me at chess, I hate to say."

"Can't she go into Nuclear Engineering?" Slade questioned. "I mean it's an honorable profession, but it can be very dangerous especially on what you're doing."

"No…no." Gary stammered.

"Okay, okay." Slade acquiesced while stepping back a few paces.

"Now where were we–oh yes. My parents owned an import export business and could afford to send me to the University of Chicago to help me quench my thirst for Nuclear Engineering. After all, that's where it basically started all those years ago. I quickly received my bachelor degree, in the field, in 30 months, and then I was surprised by receiving a very good scholarship to study at the Massachusetts Institute of Technology (MIT) for my graduate work. So with the financial help from my parents I entered the Quantum Theory and Fission technology programs. I finished my Thesis in a little over a year, and looked forward to entering one of their PhD programs. But first I took some time off and went back home for my daughter's Batmizvah. It was nice seeing my wife and daughter again, and I missed them dearly. But my studies were not yet completed and so off I went again to Boston. I just had enough time to unpack before I entered the program.

"What was your field of study?" Slade asked.

Gary thought for a moment before he answered. "Well of course I continued with Quantum Mechanics, but added AI and Nano Technology to the mix."

"My word you must have been studying day and night with a load like that." Jake said as he and Slade looked at each other.

"I was, but I was in love with my material and so it didn't really matter. I was young and full of energy and stamina."

"What was your dissertation like?" both soldiers asked.

"The program took me longer than I liked. You see a dissertation is usually a long essay on a particular subject. Usually you need to go before a board or committee, if you will, to answer questions on the essay you wrote. In my case it took almost four years of continuous study and research to complete the dissertation. Like I said, I was studying and researching on not one particular subject, but three of them. I had to know how Quantum Mechanics worked with Nano Technology and how it fit into the equation to get the most efficiency and power from Artificial Intelligence (AI). Also I wanted to know how each one, if melded to another would operate. In other words how powerful the three would be, if working together in harmony. No sooner I completed the program I was beckoned back to Israel to help my country advance in the nuclear age. I was part of the team that developed, designed and tested the Iron Dome, which both of you know is quite successful. Oh and later I want to discuss with you the United States misgivings and more of my education. Now you need to know more and understand how we are going to shut down Mother Russia's nuclear capabilities?" Both Delta Ops nodded their heads.

THIRTY-SIX

Sea Going Nuclear Submarine Technology II

Gary began to slowly pace around the big round table before speaking about submarine communication. It was more complicated than land based, because of the way speed and direction of sound traveled in this environment. "Communication with submarines is a field within military communications that presents technical challenges and requires specialized technology. Because land based radio waves do not travel well through good electrical conductors such as salt water. The submerged submarines are cut off from radio communications with their command authorities at ordinary radio frequencies. Submarines can surface and raise their antennas above the sea level, or float tethered buoys carrying an antenna, and then use regular radio transmission. However, this makes them vulnerable to detection by anti-submarine warfare forces."

Slade was fascinated on this subject and asked, "how all of this came about."

"Well let's. see" Gary said as he was thinking about where to start. "Early submarines during World War II mostly travelled on the surface because of their limited underwater speed and endurance. They dived mainly to evade immediate detection and threats or for stealthy approach to their targets. Later on nuclear-powered submarines were developed that could stay submerged for months.

Now if the atomic clock strikes 12 and we enter into a nuclear war, submerged ballistic missiles submarines have to be ordered quickly to launch their weapons. And in some rare cases, these warriors of the water may not even know what is going on, depending on where they are and if they haven't been communicated to.

Jake stepped in and offered a side of information saying," a friend of his was stationed on a nuclear submarine and found that it was large enough to give each seamen comfortable quarters."

"Yes they were not like the World War II submarines with their tight quarters smelling of smoke and diesel. Now transmitting messages to these submarines is an active area of research. Very low frequency (VLF) radio wave can penetrate seawater just over one hundred feet. Many navies use powerful shore VLF transmitters for communication. A few nations have built transmitters which use extremely low frequency (ELF) radio waves, which can penetrate seawater to reach submarines at operating depths, but these require huge antennas. Further, other techniques have been used that include sonar and blue lasers."

"What are blue lasers" Jake asked, while rubbing his burnished blond wavy hair.

"You would have to ask me that. I don't know much about this except to say it is based on electromagnetic radiation and I believe it can be seen in the water at operating depth. Now another way is acoustic transmission. Sound travels far better in water, and underwater loudspeakers and hydrophones can cover quite a gap. Apparently, both the American (SOSUS)–Sound Surveillance System, and the Russian navies have placed sonic communication equipment in the seabed of areas frequently travelled by their submarines and connected it by underwater communication cables to their land stations. If a submarine hides near such a device, it can stay in contact with its headquarters. An underwater telephone called Gertrude is also used to communicate with submarines. The name is taken from the era when switchboard operators were active.

Some of our communications may need to be copied and used for Russian communication. Of course, it will be in the language and proper dialect and this will depend on who is commanding their sub. Now the ELF coding used for U.S. military ELF transmission employed a Reed-Solomon error correction code using 64 symbols, each represented by a very long pseudo-random sequence. To make it more difficult the entire transmission was encrypted. The advantage of such a technique are that correlating multiple transmissions, a message could be completed even with a very low signal-to-noise ratios.

Because of this only a very few pseudo-random sequences represented actual message characters, if so, there was a very high chance that if a message was successfully received, it was a valid message. In other words it was not spoofed.

The communication link was one way–land based to the sea going submarine. It was a very slow way of communication and it undoubtedly was used to establish a different form of communication–usually two-way.

Getting back to a surfaced submarine, or s submarine floating a tethered buoy on the surface, one can use ordinary communications. From the surface, submarines may use naval frequencies in the HF, VHF, and UHF bands, and transmit information via both voice and teleprinters modulation techniques. Where available, dedicated military communication satellite systems using line-of-sight frequencies are preferred for long distance communications, as High Frequency (HF) are more likely to betray the location of the submarine. Recently, a couple of MIT grads have found a new way for submarines to communicate with aircraft. I think we beat this to death, but I believe it is vitally important for you to understand how this all works in case something happens to me."

"Nothing's going to happen to you. We got you covered." Both soldiers said.

THIRTY-SEVEN

Land Based Communication

"**I**'ll keep this pretty brief fellas. You know most of them anyway. I'm going to start with tactical based radios that the military uses. The five forms of land based communication for the military is radio, satellite, telephone, computer and visual. The military alphabet starts with Alpha and ends with Zulu. Why am I telling you this, you guys use it all the time. Satellite communication is based on line of sight. Of course if you transmit the message to the next satellite in line you extend the line of sight. This is just an introduction, but are we covered fellas?' Oh, one other thing we also have the police band radio system like 10-4 is okay and 10-8 I believe is in service, and 10-7 is out of service. The military alphabet was first used in World War II. The civilian police code was first used in the 1950s I believe.

"Oh, another thing for land communication and invented quite recently. It's called ShotSpotter. It's a gunshot detection system that uses acoustic sensors to triangulate where a shot or shots originates from and then wirelessly alert the police. It can be attached to almost anything. It has now been improved to the point to not only alert police where the shot(s) came from, but also identify the caliber of the weapon and in some cases identify the brand. It's a very useful tool for police. Before, police would receive multiple phone calls from concerned citizens that they heard shot(s), and in most cases they weren't sure where it came from or on the other hand intentional misguided information. I heard recently that Chicago were taking down their devices. I guess they were hearing so much information coming in they couldn't keep up."

"Ya, I heard other cities are doing the same. What are we coming to?" Slade said, shaking his head. "I just hope the new Trump Administration can turn things around. The President only has four years to undo the damage of the previous administration, and he'll need all the help he can get to get the job done. I can see why we are preparing to do this in case President Trump and Putin don't see eye-to-eye. We don't need any tactical nukes fired off let alone the big boys being discharged. Jake and I already know about the newer technology where bees and insects can fly around and take photos and record sound and then send them back to their commanding officer. That's a great tool for the military. If things get much worse here, Congress will have to enact new laws to do this domestically.

THIRTY-EIGHT

Pre-Planning

"According to what we've identified, there are two land-based nuclear missile installations that are not digital. The first one is Yerma Epema. It is approximately 1550 miles deep into central Russia from Moscow. It's an older installation housing SS-19s and they are liquid propelled vehicles generally pointing toward the U. S. aim points." Gary said, as he was rubbing the back of his neck.

"I just spoke with James and his staff, and Ernie will get three railway vouchers for us first thing tomorrow." Jake said.

"Why train ticket?." Slade groaned while spinning a Russian rouble coin on the table.

"The boss wants to make sure we look like tourists enjoying some of Russia's scenery. We'll get there in a couple of days and then we can reconnoiter the installation." Jake said as he gave Slade a sideways glance.

"Gary, is Yuri alright. I mean he isn't spooked because of all the news about the break in at one of the buildings at Moscow State University?" Jake asked.

"No, he's fine." Gary said while thinking about the operation.

"When is he going to get us the latest schematic for the silo?" Slade inquired.

"At the hotel we will be staying at in Yerma." Gary responded.

"Well I hope so, because the clock is ticking." Slade commented.

In the meantime, since everyone had the highest level of security, Jake tested it by getting the coordinates to the nearest keyhole satellite, over Yerma, and signed in. He downloaded the photos and information. The city, rather the town, was quite small with about three thousand in population. The terrain was mostly flat with a few hills nearby. The three gathered that about a third of the town's population were military, and were there for maintenance and upkeep of the installation while the rest of the population were secondary and served the military.

They updated the scan of the area, in order to see the silo with its dull gray doors. There was Russian language written along the edges. The satellite's photos were so clear that Gary could read the inscriptions. He told Jake and Slade it mostly said to stay away and do not try to open the doors. Gary went on and told the two delta ops what they were dealing with. "The old SS-19's were part of a series that started with the SS-17s, SS-18s, SS-19s and SS-20s. They were about 24 meters long, 2.5 meters wide and their launch weight was about 105,000 kg. They were in the 600 kilo ton (kt) range and were the first to be equipped with Multiple Independent Reentry Vehicle (MIRV)warheads, and there were six of them. However, they all fired at the same time and hit the same locations. They weren't dynamic in nature as with the newer technology. They used two stage liquid propellants for their propulsion, and had a range of about 8,500 miles. Even though they don't measure up to today's mega ton load, they are still quite deadly and can do serious damage to a mid-size city.

THIRTY-NINE

Traveling

J ake knew that any of the three could have gotten the train vouchers. But why be photographed and possibly discovered. Even though it has been a few days since the MSU fiasco, why take any chances. Sure, there is always the risk of being followed, but after a few days and all the heat from the real source finding nothing, the odds are high that they haven't been located. Knowing the Russkies if they knew where they were, the jig would already been up. Also the propaganda on the news channels, especially TASS, RIA, Novosti, and the rest of the news organizations was almost laughable to the point of being ludicrous. Everyone had their own story and conspirators were alive and well. Even though President Putin tried to contain it, the news was known worldwide. The United States was conjecturing and gaslighting its populace like there was no tomorrow. *It's ironic,* Jake thought. *Here the three were trying to extend tomorrow, not shorten it.*

When Ernie got back with the vouchers all three were pleasantly surprised that James splurged a little on the taxpayers' dole and got all three of them separate VIP (CB) class carriages arranged on separate cars for security purposes. The branded long distance trains were like our AMTRACK with amenities ranging from VIP (CB) to third class called platskart. The platskart was like sleeping in a large dorm room with bunks. If you value economy over comfort that's your choice. Although it can get quite noisy in there so bring your ear plugs. The VIP (CB) passengers had their own dining car and menu which was quite extensive. Diners were treated to fine chinaware, heavy silver plated utensils and fancy glassware like Waterford. The spirit, wine and beer menus were first rate. And Stoli was given free gratis to CB passengers. The meals were superb and made right there. CB passengers also had their own bar and cigar room they called reading rooms. They even had their own observation car

"

with wrap-around glass for excellent viewing…Their CB carriages came with comfortable beds with brand name pillows, downs and sheets. Each car had 24 hour news and internet. Of course the internet was blocked from certain sources. They had their own showers and even bars for entertainment.

When Slade learned of all the amenities, he was all smiles again. "I guess the boss felt sorry for us and wanted us to be comfortable."

"I wish I was going with you guys," Ernie quipped. "It sounds more like a vacation than a trip."

"I wouldn't be too happy yet, fellas," Jake counseled. "We may be heading into a maelstrom and James knows it. He just wants us to have some down time before the proverbial hits you know what."

FORTY

Yerma

After the three tourist departed the small train station in town and headed for the Euro hotel, Slade remarked to Jake what an odd name for an hotel in the middle of Russia.

"The developer must have had a spoonful of vodka when naming the structure." Jake quipped. "But I must say, even though it is small, the facade of the building is beautiful. From our orders, it says the hotel was built during the Stalin era. I can't wait to check in and see what our rooms are alike. I'm sure James scattered the rooms throughout the hotel for security reasons."

"Isn't it a bit odd that three tourists traveling together have rooms not together?" Slade asked.

"Naw, not really. The staff doesn't care, they're just doing their jobs. Besides, remember were not checking in at the same time. "

"That's true." Slade remarked. "Who's first?"

"You're looking at him."

"Of course, I should have known that." Slade remarked with a smirk on his face.

"Okay let's go." Jake said. "I'll keep you guys in touch via sat phone."

After all three checked in they met in Jake's room. It was actually a two room suite with chairs and a table in the second room. Nothing fancy, but it served their purpose.

"How come you get the best accommodations?" Slade whined again ribbing his friend in his side. "You have all the luck."

Jake ignored Slade's antics and asked, "Okay, what do we have, Gary?" looking at the much smaller bespectacled man.

"Just got the most recent schematics and information from Yuri an hour ago." Gary said while he rolled out a couple of schematics on the table showing the installation. "It's interesting to note that the Russian technicians live five miles away from the silo. I think this is for their safety, because there may be radiation leaks around the installation."

"Did Yuri leave us a Geiger?" Slade asked, with a little concern.

"Ya he did. It's in my room." Gary responded.

"I wonder how many of the town's people have cancer and aren't aware of it." Jake said to no one in particular. "Being in Russia is one of those drawbacks and these people here suffer the consequences, and this is probably happening in various other places in Russia with land based nukes. Look at what happened in Chernobyl."

"Hold on just a minute, Jake." Gary said. "We won't know until we Geiger the installation. Yuri said we need to find the remote to open the maintenance door beside the silo in order to get in."

"Gary, aren't you forgetting something?"

"Oh ya, the six-foot cyclone fence studded with razor wire."

"The satellite photos show that the fence has a rather stout metal lock on the gate. Did Yuri bring a key for the gate" Jake asked.

"No I don't believe so."

'How about the maintenance schedules?" Jake asked, looking around the room again.

"Why do you ask?" Gary quizzed with an odd look on his narrow face. He felt like he was being interrogated.

"Well first of all it would tell us how often the maintenance crew worked on the installation. Since there is a very small chance we will ever find the key or remote for the door we'll have to break in. So it would be nice to know how often these guys show up. My gut feeling is they really don't follow the maintenance schedule because of possible radiation danger. That's the reason why they live five miles away. Besides the silo is out in the middle of nowhere and who's to check." Jake rationed.

"Good point." Gary concurred.

The group then studied the interior of the silo and the machinery involved. Yuri got them excellent schematics and information on how the equipment worked. After a lengthy study session, they determined the most direct and simple way of shutting down the silo. In other words they followed Occam's Razor. They also had the logic decipher equipment based on Quantum Mechanics to neutralize the six keys that enabled launching the missile. Tomorrow, they agreed to reconnoiter the installation perimeter and bring Mr. Geiger along to check for radiation. They found a good restaurant in town and had an old fashion Russian meal of borst, boiled potatoes and beets. They even had a little Stoli. After all, when in Russia you do what the Russians do–drink vodka.

FORTY-ONE

Tomorrow

They were up early and heading out when Gary checked his jacket and said, "hold on" to the two delta ops. "What's wrong?" Jake inquired with a concerned look on his face.

"I forgot Mr. Geiger." Gary said.

"Okay, you see that shop over there." Jake pointed.

"Sure." Gary said.

"Slade and I will hang over there."

"Be right back"

While Gary was gone, the two delta ops looked at one of the schematics again. They were about a mile from the site and the trek would give them a better feel of what Yerma was like. The diagram indicated there was a six foot cyclone fence with razor wire sitting atop. It wound around the perimeter of the facility with a locking metal gate on the east side of the complex. When the time came it wouldn't be a problem getting in with a good set of bolt cutters. And they wouldn't be too choosy about how they got in, because they wouldn't be there for long. Once their business was done, Yuri would be back with train vouchers to the other site. Today was only to check things out. Jake wanted to know the general appearance of the silo. This would give him some indication of what condition the installation was like and hence how often the soldiers were there. Also, they needed to know what Mr. Geiger said in milliroentgens (mRs). Both Delta Force soldiers knew that it was a unit of measure when multiplied by hours and years would tell them how much they could safely withstand. By Jake's thinking the higher the mRs the less time the Russian maintenance crew would visit the site.

"Aw, you're back, buddy." Jake said with a twinkle in his blue eyes. "Boy this thing is heavy," Gary lamented.

"Here, give to me," Slade said in his usual gravelly voice.

Gary handed the device to Slade and looked around while Slade put it in his knapsack.

"Okay, let's head out," Jake said impatiently.

It was 9am on a Sunday and a half of Yerma was still snoozing while the other half were in church. The air was crisp and very cold and sound traveled easily through the nearby hills. There was a smattering of snow on the ground and the soldiers used some nearby tree limbs once they got out of town to disguise their tracks. They didn't want anyone to know where they were heading.

"The town seemed fine," Gary remarked. "It's like any small town in Israel and I bet the U.S."

"It is, and the only thing I don't like about it is it's too blasted cold and the winters are long." Slade intervened. "However, they drink a lot of vodka and snooze all winter long." Everyone chuckled at that.

Jake looked back at the town. It now looked smaller then when they were in town, and they were climbing. "Heads up everyone, where getting close." Jake cautioned. "Slade get Geiger out and start taking base readings."

"Okay boss man, will do."

"Gary, keep disguising your tracks." Jake said as he looked around. He could see the cyclone fence in the distance with its bristling razor wire seeming to move from the cold Siberian wind. "Is it getting colder or is it my imagination?" Jake asked.

"It's dropped 5 degrees Fahrenheit since we left town and now its 5 below zero." Gary said as he shrugged deeper into his heavy winter coat.

"And this is only November!" Slade exclaimed, stomping his boots.

"What's Mr. Geiger say?" Jake questioned.

"The mRs are pretty high for a base reading." Slade announced as he was looking down at the meter. "Look at the cyclone fence," he said. "It's twisted and torn in places. Anyone could just walk through."

"And look," Jake said, peering closely at the fence. "There are rust marks showing along the length of the fence. Let's keep going around the perimeter. I want to get a good look at everything. What's the Geiger counter say?"

"It's going up even more," Slade said with a worried look on his face.

They all stopped at the gate to see what kind of lock they were dealing with.

"Piece of cake," Slade said, as he peered closely at the locking mechanism.

"Okay, let's head back and get out of this cold." Jake said as he turned and started walking towards town. "I've seen enough, and the way things look, I don't think the maintenance crew has been here for at least a couple of years. I'm beginning to think the SS-19 couldn't launch even if the Russkies wanted it to. Let's go and get some hot grub and plan for the take down.

FORTY-TWO

Downtime

"When do you think we need to go up there again?" Gary inquired.

"We're not in any hurry, are we guys?" Jake said with his crooked smile. "Besides let's study the schematics again to make sure we haven't missed anything. I kind of like this little town—the foods' good and the people are friendly and accommodating."

Slade looked at friend and couldn't believe what he just said. *This isn't like him,* Slade thought. He usually likes to get the job done and get out of Dodge. "Okay, what's going on my friend?" Slade queried with his gravelly voice.

"Well I've got my eye on a gorgeous Russian brunette and she sure looks yummy."

Slade's dark eyes went full circle looking at his friend. "You can't do that. You'd be breaking a cardinal rule, and what about Zoey?"

"Just kidding my friend, just kidding. You know I would never do that, Zoey or no Zoey. I'd be putting the whole assignment in jeopardy, not to mention the people involved. I'd find myself out on the streets without a job. But you know I think we do need a little downtime to determine the buzz going on in this town. What'll think guys?"

"You're the boss my friend and you know what's best." Gary quipped.

The three kept a low profile for the next couple of days, and sometimes ate together while other times alone. They didn't get to chummy with anyone and kept their ears and eyes wide open. They didn't learn anything except they were new in town. Jake updated the plan with James and didn't find anything new from the Deputy Secretary. Next he communicated with Yuri on his encrypted sat phone and told him he would contact him when he needed the train vouchers for their next destination. You couldn't reserve train tickets in advance in Russia.

FORTY-THREE

Getting There

On Wednesday morning Yuri showed up with the train vouchers and special permits for the town of Severodvinsk, their next destination. It was nearly 4,000 miles away from Yerma, and much more populated with 192,000 citizens and major military installations were there. The city was north of Arkhangelsk Oblast, Russia. It was in the Delta of the Northern Dvina River, 22 miles west of Arkhangelsk and near the White Sea. It was the administrative center of the oblast. Due to the presence of important military shipyards specializing in developing submarines, the special permits were required. Once again, Gary came through with an old Russian friend, Dimitri Petrov, whom he met on several occasions while attending nuclear science conferences in Russia. He provided additional information.

"Gary, where are you getting all of your friends from?" Jake questioned with concern creeping into his voice.

"Didn't you read my dossier?" Gary quipped.

"Sure did and I didn't find anything that would allow you easy access to Russia."

"Well my friend it so happens that I have dual citizenship. My dad's last name was Zimmerman, and my mother's name is Katya Romanova. Zimmerman in Hebrew means a carpenter. And of course my Russian side means, 'a woman from a royal family.'"

"Are you a direct descendent of the Romanov Dynasty on your mother's side?" Jake asked with wonderment in his voice.

"Yup, sure am."

"Well I'll be a monkey's uncle," Jake said, shaking his head. "Hey Slade did you know about this?"

"Of course, it was in his dossier."

"Well I better get my head screwed on straight before I lose it," Jake said, still shaking it.

Slade dug into the envelope containing the train vouchers. and what he saw made his steely black eyes twinkle, and a wide smile broke out all over his gruff face. CB in big bold beautiful letters graced all three tickets. "Bingo!" he yelled.

Gary and Jake both turned to Slade with surprise looks on their faces. Jake was the first to speak. "What's going on Slade, you sound like you just hit the jackpot."

"Ya, Slade, you been playing the Russian lottery games?"

"I might as will be!" Slade exclaimed. He held up the three vouchers so his friends could see 'CB' printed on them.

"Oh that," Jake feinted.

"That's no big deal," Gary chimed in.

Slade looked at his two friends with an incredulous look on his face and shook his head. "Are you guys crazy? I mean we'll be treated like kings for eight days getting to Severodvinsk."

Gary and Jake broke out in earth shaking laughter, and Jake had to hold his gut before he and Gary collapsed on the couch. Slade looked at the pair and it wasn't long before he motioned them to make room, as all three busted out laughing at the top of their lungs while lollygagging on the couch.

"Okay enough of this," Jake said with all seriousness in his deep blue eyes. He rubbed his burnished blonde locks thinking he needed that. It was 10am and they needed to get going. He looked at Gary and asked if he had Mr. Geiger. He nodded. They checked the camera feed again from the cameras they imbedded on their first trip and there wasn't any activity.

"Okay boys let's pack up and get going. The sooner we get done, the sooner we can board our carriage to Severodvinsk."

Slade gave a big nod while a huge smile broke out on his face. He couldn't wait!

FORTY-FOUR

The Take Down

The trio took a little different path this time to allay any suspicion. The weather was warmer today at about a cherry 10 degrees. The three wasted no time getting to the east side of the complex where Jake quickly cut through the lock with a pair of bolt cutters. They carefully went to the silo door looking for any surprises, such as I.E.Ds on the way. Once at the gray metal door, Jake studied it cautiously to see if there were any nasty packages. There was nothing. Jake collected a big piece of wood nearby and told everyone to stand back while he tested the door. It was solid. He looked at the lock again and it looked ordinary. Next he checked the edges of the door to see if he could somehow jimmy the door—no such luck. "Hey, Slade hand me the portable blow torch. I'm going to cut through the lock."

He was sure happy that Yuri mailed the equipment to the hotel ahead of time. Without it he wasn't sure if they could get in.

After it was done, Jake stood at the opening eye-balling the interior to see if anything caught his eye. It all looked like cold war architecture wrapped in corrugated aluminum cylinders with about a fifteen foot diameter to transfer the large machinery to the bottom. Jake looked down the hole with his powerful LED light and saw that there was a ladder welded to the side of the corrugated metal and it followed all the way down another three levels. The three climbed down to see what was there. As they entered the control room they saw nothing except Cold War apparatus. The place was very dark and spooky with more Cold War equipment surrounding them. In those days things were always large. Along the way Jake checked for motion detectors, infrared sensors with his meter and anything else that looked out of sorts. To him everything looked out of sorts. He was looking at equipment from a different era—probably the 70s. For its time everything seemed normal looking including the enormous missile. They were now in the center of the control room, 200 feet below the surface. Slade looked around with his LED high intensity light and found a light switch on the control room wall and viola there was light albeit a little dark because of the old incandescent light bulb. The main engine slid below the concrete floor they were standing on..

Two thirds of the monster was in cased in an gantry with four gate/clamps on each side that broke away when the main engine fired and the missile began to move. There was an small metal railing that encircled the missile at the opening of the concrete floor to protect anyone from falling in. Slade could see candy and food wrappers laying around. He walked over to the program desk and studied the launch controls. By then Jake put his LED flashlight away since Slade found the switch to lighten the interior. Jake looked around again with the room being lit this time and again he didn't see anything out of order. He motioned Gary over to the control desk and asked, "What do you think?"

Gary peered at the desk and controls, and then checked his information and compared the control desk to one of the schematics from Yuri. They were almost identical except for the placement of the two launch keys. "Everything looks good, but we shouldn't touch anything yet, because the control system could be rigged."

"I hear ya." Jake intoned. He took out a bomb schematic showing possible scenarios for C4 explosives and newer explosives, such as PETN and IMX-101. He got down on his knees, pulled out his LED flashlight and looked at the underside of the desk to see if he could spot anything, and he did. It was a case clamped to the underside with double wires extending up to the mechanical equipment which was part of the launch control. He got back up and told Gary to go outside until Slade and he could disarm the device.

"What is it?" Gary asked, with a terrible look on his narrow face.

"We don't know yet. So step outside and put some distance between you and the silo. We'll let you know when it's okay to come back in."

After Gary left, Slade turned to his boss and asked, "What do you think?"

"First, let's check Mr. Geiger again."

Slade pulled out the device from his knapsack and checked the meter. "Holy mackerel!" He shrieked, looking at his boss to see if he was glowing.

"That bad, huh?" Jake said, looking at his friend in alarm.

"Well, I know Gary is safe because the explosive nature of the device can't be too powerful, or it would destroy the back end of the missile, and he's away from the higher mR readings. Shall we begin my good boy?" Jake asked while eyeing the package.

"Ya, let's get this done and fast. We don't want to start glowing by the time we start our trip back." They both got down and started their testing and work. They disarmed the sensors first and then opened the device door to see what exactly they had. They suspected correctly. The configuration spelled IMX-101 a new explosive, but just as powerful as C4. However, it wasn't as sensitive to explosives containing nitroglycerin. They both drew in a breath of relief when they saw what they had. They finished disarming the device and then called Gary to come back in.

Gary looked at both soldiers and could see they were pretty tensed. "What's going on?" He asked.

"You want the good or the bad first." Slade requested with his low gravelly voice.

Gary examined his friends closely. *They weren't kidding,* he thought. "Okay, I'll bite for the bad."

"We need to work fast, or we'll start glowing like a florescent stick." Jake uttered, rubbing his hands together.

"That bad, huh." Without waiting for an answer, he asked the next question. "And the good?"

"We found IMX-101 explosives," Slade responded.

"What's that?" Gary asked, as he was still looking at the two Delta ops.

"It's a newer explosive and less sensitive than most, and that's good." Jake said.

Gary thought about this for a moment and understood. "I guess it's my turn at bat to figure out the launching system."

"Hit a home run, my friend. We need to do this quickly because the soldiers or someone came in and changed the explosives recently. We saw other marks on the underside that indicated a larger and perhaps more powerful and more sensitive device." Jake responded, still studying the package that he and Slade just defanged.

FORTY-FIVE

Gary's Turn

G ary stepped up to the plate and began investigating the control panel. He saw that it was an old double action control system which required two people to launch the missile. In between the two key slots was a four digit count down system, like an old slot machine. *He has seen these before,* he thought. He took out a kit that contained a very powerful light and magnification system. The system was somewhat similar to what an Ophthalmologist uses, but much more powerful. He had the ability to use multiple illuminations while using different magnifications simultaneously. He inspected the entire control system and couldn't find any back door. "No luck here, Jake," Gary lamented. "It looks like there is no way to electronically or logically disarm the system. Plus, I highly doubt that there is a remote system that alerts the maintenance crew if anyone tinkers with it. I guess it's cutting time and hope they don't discover this until we disarm their entire nuclear capability."

"Okay, will cut out the entire launch system, carry it someplace, bury it and let the snow take care of the rest. This all clunker is going to take a couple of trips of us working together. So let's store our gear here." Jake took out his torch and started while the other two held visquene around the cutting area to reduce sparks from flying everywhere. After he was finished, Slade and him kick the control system off the desk to the concrete floor. Jake then cut the launch system in half and all three stood back and waited for the cutting marks to cool. They found an old bucket in the corner of the control room. They filled it with snow and buried it on the hot edges. They did this several times to help the cooling process. They wanted to get the heck out of Dodge. *So far so good,* Jake thought. After the cooling they all collected a chunk of the old launch control system, and walked a quarter of a mile. While Jake was using his military shovel to make a shallow grave in the frozen ground, Gary and

Slade walked back to get the rest of the old control system. After they arrived, they buried all the remains, including the extra equipment, in the shallow grave. They moved snow over the fresh marks and bruised it with tree limbs as best they could until the snow did the rest. They tree limbed their way back to the silo, collected their equipment and trekked back to town. Jake thought, *It probably didn't matter, anyway. The theft probably wouldn't be discovered for at least a year, seeing how lazy the soldiers were.*

FORTY-SIX

The Train Ride

After getting back, they all cleaned up, packed their clothes and equipment and went to the hotel's small restaurant to get a bite to eat before making their way to the train station.

Jake looked around the carriage station and found nothing unusual and waited for Gary to show up. After he arrived, they then waited a little longer for Slade to come in. They all waited in different sections of the station until their train arrived.

Slade was the first to check in and go to his cabin without a word from the other two. Jake and Gary followed going to their cabins. They arranged and stowed their belongings before making their way to the observation car. Again, it was well furnished with wrap-around glass showing the Russian country side. It was great and the glass stayed clear of snow, because of something the train's maintenance crew used.

"That seemed almost too easy guys. I'm still leery that someone is following us." Jake said.

"Oh come on, can't you ever relax. Slade ribbed his partner. "Let's all order s Stoli and a beer chaser. You know it's included in our fare."

"Ya, I know, but you never know."

"I know what's wrong with you," Slade said, smiling."

"What's that?" Jake quizzed.

"It's all those wonderful babes you have. It won't be long before Christmas and you can celebrate."

"I don't have all those babes anymore as you call them. Remember I have been with Zoey for the last couple of years. That reminds me, I better call her here while I have a chance."

Jake moved to the end of the car to make the call as Gary was coming in from the restroom. His Stoli shot and beer was waiting for him.

"I hope you don't mind," Slade said. "It's time to relax a little. We have a long trip to Severodvinsk, and I can't wait to go over the Urals. I hear the view is really nice. Although, this time of year, everything will be white because of all the snow."

"Ya it will and lots of it. Shalom my friend.!" They clinked glasses and downed their Stoli. While working on their beers Gary was curious about the affairs of the United States and asked, "what's going on with Congress? I mean they are blaming each other for all the mistakes and lies that have been going on for at least the last twenty years. It seems as though the only thing important to them is winning. You now essentially have two sides warring against each other for power and to hell with the people. They spend money like drunken sailors and sometimes on themselves for the most idiotic things. I was thinking the other day that they probably don't care if they run out of the taxpayers' money, or the taxpayers quit paying their taxes, because they can fire up the printing presses anytime they like and print more money. Although, over time, the United States currency will lose its place as the globes most trusted and number one legal tender. By then inflation will be entrenched for some time, and I bet it will be in the triple digit range like some of the banana republics. I just think things are really getting out of hand. And this is just the tip of the iceberg. I know our country, Israel, has their own troubles, but nothing like this"

"Slade sat back in in his strato-lounger and thought for a long time before answering. "You know what you just said, might be right. Gary. As I see it, we are just finishing the worst administration I have seen in my entire life. And right now I hate to say it, but I'm really upset and embarrassed with our country. Quite frankly, because of Biden's age and health, I believe his administration is basically being run and orchestrated by some of his senior level staff, and don't forget about the auto-pen. I'm sorry to say this, but the man is senile as the day is long and just as crooked. He has been in public life, mainly the senate, for fifty years and has not made his mark on anything. It's really a shame; because I think when all is said and done he can be a pretty nice guy.

In fact, I think most of if not all his family lives in the same flavor. Like I said we don't have a President running the country anymore; just his administration and cronies. Right now, we are easy pickins'. The only thing saving us is our massive nuclear capability. and it's too easy to push a button."

"I hear ya Slade. There's a guy I know pretty well, his name is Frank Mulligan."

"I think he's been on CNN or Fox, probably both. I knew him from the days when Israel had some financial matters with First Steel Bank of New York. Frank was the CFO. I believe the finances had something to do with Israel building the Iron Dome. He didn't come up with a pedigree on his back, or any Ivy League schools, like most executive officers at his bank. Oh no, he rolled up his shirt sleeves and came up the hard way, and he is sharper than a finely honed butcher's knife. At least forty years on the butcher block from a junior loan officer at Benjamin Franklin Savings and Loan. I believe those were in the days when consumers could assume existing loans, and their paper wasn't being sold. The word on the street is he told Jack Scanner, his CEO at First Steel Bank to stuff it. He knew about Jack's malfeasance at his former company. He was tired of fending off his boss's crazy accounting schemes, especially during the 07, 08 Tarp era dilemma. Oh yes! Gary exclaimed. He's the MAN if you want to know about your countries machinations, and there are so many of them. You can find him in Path To Peril."

Slade thought for a long moment and wondered why Gary was so interested in the United States. "What's going on here?" Slade asked. "Why are you so interested in our country's affairs?"

"Come on, buddy!" Gary huffed. "Don't you know Israel's fortunes are directly tied to your nation. I mean without you backing us up, the Middle East would totally be on fire and a catalyst to WW III."

" I suppose so," Slade responded.

"There's no suppose so about it." Gary said, shaking his head. "I'll have a lot more to say about this later. If you don't mind I'm going to grab one of these cushions, get comfy and drift away for a while."

"Be my guest." About then Jake came back after talking with Zoey. Slade looked up to his friend and ask, " how she was doing?"

"Zoey is doing great," Jake remarked. "She is getting ready for Christmas and can't wait until she can see me again. She and Jane, her younger sister, went to Hawaii awhile back for two weeks and they both had to keep the men at bay while they were getting nice tans and having a great time."

"Where were they staying?"

"For them, Oahu of course. They thought about taking a hop to Maui, but Jane was against it. She was skittish about seeing all the fire damage that had occurred. So they just stayed around Oahu and tempted the boys. Slade, you haven't met Jane yet since we have been so busy, but she is an absolute dish, and very intelligent too. I'm not sure I want to introduce her to you yet."

"Well this is the first time I even heard of her?" Slade mused, smiling at his friend. "So in the short term you don't have to worry, but in the long term it could be "watch out!" But first, Jane, will have to get past my two protective daughters, Marla and Darla."

Jake looked across the aisle and ask how Gary was doing. "Poor guy, he's totally knock out from all the activity going on. I know this isn't the quickest way to get to Severodvinsk, but the boss was probably right to give us some down time while traveling." Slade surmised.

"Ya, James has the confidence in us that the job was done right in Yerma and they will probably not find anything until the maintenance crew arrives again, and who knows when. Besides, we made it look like the locals did it." Jake responded. "Meth heads, you know."

Next morning they all met in the dining room and had a wonderful breakfast topped with rich Turkish Mocha Valley espresso.

"How you feeling?" Slade asked looking at Gary.

"Slept like a baby guys. The Russians sure know how to make a comfortable bed for CB travelers. Got up and had a nice hot shower and put on some clean clothes. I feel great and now I'm ready to enjoy the rest of our trip before we arrive in Severodvinsk.

FORTY-SEVEN

Any News Is Good News

Damian Petrov sat back in his chair and thought about what they were doing. The FSB agents were now scouring Russia far and wide, including all the military districts, if that's possible for a country this big. The net was greatly expanded after learning there were three tourist, supposedly, in Yerma. Unfortunately, the town was so small there were no cameras anywhere. They had to rely on what the town's folks had said, and that was practically nothing. The hotel where they were staying only looked at their credentials and didn't take any photos of them. *What a bunch of idiots*, he thought. After all, it's just a podunk town in the middle of nowhere. What would they know? Well, at least they discovered they had train vouchers traveling to Severodvinsk. They could possibly stop the train, but really they had no evidence to do so. He wondered why they were going there. He remembered it was a heavy industrial city that was a good place to work. *Wait a minute,* he thought. *Aren't there a couple of shipyards there that are developing and manufacturing nuclear submarines?* He'd make a few inquiries to get a better handle on the sub bases. Could these three people be heading there to gain information on the latest design or possibly sabotage the place?

He checked, and because of the importance of the sub bases everyone who had business or visiting there had to pass through security zones in order to travel around the city. After conferring with one of the lead commandants at the largest shipyard he learned, indeed, they are developing and building state of the art submarines for the Russian Navy. He warned the commandant to inform their security around the base for three people that may be snooping around. The commandant was a little upset with the special agent, because he didn't know anything about them except their general appearance. And that could easily be changed.

After the commandant broke the connection he hoped that Damien Petrov would call him back with more information soon, so he could alert his security forces. Sometimes he wandered about the FSB. *For Christ's sake,* he thought, *are they slipping a notch or two?*

FORTY-EIGHT

The Urals

The Ural Mountains in Russia are a long mountainous range stretching north-south through Western Russia acting as the traditional boundary between Europe and Asia. They are known for their rich mineral deposits including iron ore, copper, gold and gemstones, and are considered one of the world's oldest mountain ranges, formed by the collision of ancient continental plates. The highest peak is Mount Narodnaya, reaching 6,217 feet in elevation. The northern slopes are forested with tundra and lots of Evergreens composed of Douglas Fir, Hemlock and some Dogwoods and Maple. The southern part is mainly grassland. Their carriage would cut across the northern part of the range. The closer they got, the more excited Slade became.

"What's with you?" Jake asked, shaking his head. "You would've thought Christmas was already here. Besides, the higher we go the more snow we encounter. It won't be long before we won't see anything except white."

"You know I have Russian in me." Slade explained.

"So what." Jake said, shaking his head. "A lot of people have Russian in them. Look at Gary, he's half Russian and from a royal family at that."

"Well some of my ancestors came from this region a few hundred years ago. And even though it was a long time ago, I have never seen the hills they tilled until now."

"Is that why you are growing a beard to mimic your ancestors," Jake kidded. "It's mostly snow you know, so you can't possibly see much."

"I don't care. Now I know I have been here."

Gary chimed in. "Okay, Jake, quit picking on my brethren–he's a good guy."

"That's right, you two are as thick as thieves," Jake said rolling his blue eyes.

"What about you, Jake?" Gary inquired.

"I'm mostly Scottish–you know, the James Bond type," and with that all three leaned back and roared. Luckily, there wasn't anyone around in the reading car to overhear their antics.

"I guess it was too early for cigars and vodka, even by Russian standards,"

Gary remarked.

"Look around it is so pillowy, soft, and hardly a…wait…do you guys see that beautiful buck standing over there? He looks so regal, just like my ancestors. I can almost hear them planning on how they would take down that beautiful animal for their next meal." Slade said, as he was looking through one of the reading car's windows.

"I hear it too," Gary said.

"I hear nothing. " Jake said as he slapped his knees. Another round of laughter and lollygagging occurred when suddenly Jake raised his hand to stop. 'I thought I heard some rustling over there pointing to it. There, do you guys hear it, too?"

"I think one of our buddies is getting a free ride," Slade said as he suddenly rushed two rows over. What happened next could only be described as hilarious. The squirrel suddenly jumped on Slade's shoulders as he was reaching for it. The two tumbled to the floor as Jake and Gary where shaking their heads, laughing boisterously just as a conductor entered the car to see what all the commotion was about. Gary pointed to the squirrel as it was scampering down the aisle for safety. The conductor laughed and told Gary they once had a brown bear enjoying their transportation system and they had to close off both ends of the car until they got to their next stop and animal control authorities took over from there. And as I understood it, it was something to watch. "Now can I get you guys anything?" the conductor asked.

"How about a round of that wonderful Mocha Valley espresso," Gary said in Russian to the conductor.

"Coming right up. Is there anything else you fellas need?" the conductor asked. "How about some running squirrel for a snack," they all laughed.

After the conductor left serving them espresso, they went to Jake's compartment getting down to business again. Their down time was nearly over as the train crested the Urals and started heading north toward

Severodvinsk. The weather was getting colder the further north they went. Most of Russia was not a kind country in the winter. A lot of areas could see temperatures in the 40 to 50 below zero range, and we are not even speaking about Siberia.

They all congregated around the room's small table as Gary laid out a map showing the old installation in northeast Severodvinsk.

"First, I want to say your Russian has greatly improved since getting here. I can tell you guys have been busy learning the language." Gary said, as he looked at the two black ops sitting opposite next to him at the table.

"It wasn't easy," Slade said. "At first I couldn't find any rhyme or reason to the language, but after a while I was finding a certain rhythm while Jake and I were practicing it. I don't know if it had anything to do with the dialect we were studying, but it kind of made since."

"Now onto the next order of business," Jake said with his deep blue eyes in heavy concentration.

FORTY-NINE

Strategy

G ary looked at Jake as he nodded his head. The ex-Delta Force ops knew how important this was if they were going to successfully complete the operation. The complex was newer than the one in Yerma, but they knew the launch system for the SS-19 was technically and mechanically the same. The problem they had was to get to it, get the job done and get out of Severodvinsk unnoticed as fast as they could. This had to be a tightly synchronized operation for it to be successful.

The city was pretty good sized and even though the silo was a few miles from the outskirts of the city, there were still people around. The trick was to create a minor distraction to allow them to dispose of the contents in a manner that it wouldn't be found quickly. The commotion couldn't be too large, or the city's transportation system would lock down. Luckily, for them there was an old industrial site nearby that would work for the disposition of the contents. However, they needed to move the control unit in one trip and a short bed truck would do the trick. Why not leave the contents in the control room and just leave. Good question, but the powers to be wanted it to look like some meth heads busted in and took the equipment with them to sell on the black market–just like Yerma. Like us, Russia had a terrible drug problem with its youth. So in one day, they had to have a truck, crudely break in, cut the control launch system out of the control desk, load it on the truck, tie it down and then drive the short distance to the old industrial site and dispose of it there. Then all three would calmly dispose the truck, hop a trolley to the security check point, get through and walk the short block to the train station. Of course the minor explosions at some of the city's companies would help them to get through unnoticed. After all this, they would board the train to St. Petersburg while a calamity was going on in the city from the distractions. Of course, they hoped there wouldn't be any surprises like there was in Yerma.

Going through the scenario that Gary described, Jake figured after deboarding the train at Severodvinsk they will have no more than eight hours to get the job done before boarding the next train to St. Petersburg.

"Gary, has Yuri left our train passes for St. Petersburg at our pre-assigned train deposit box at the train station, and how about our new credentials with Slade having a beard and Gary having hair Jake asked, as he was still running the plan through his mind.

"It's already done, Jake. We can grab the stuff when we arrive and use them for the security checkpoint. I'll go to the restroom stall and put on my wig."

"Oh you're going to look beautiful," Slade said, while laughing with Jake. "Now let's start packin', we have less than a day before we arrive. We're well rested and ready to roll," Jake said. He was still worried about the task ahead of them. Eight hours was cutting it close. As each of them returned to their cabins they were all deep in thought about the next phase of the operation. Slade knew this was a critical piece,, and it had to go off perfectly for them to succeed. He knew why he and Jake where there to help Gary. Jake already told him they would be using their military training. If needed they would adapt, improvise and modify each step as needed. They weren't renting a flatbed truck–they would steal one to cut some time out of the operation. For all they knew they needed the extra time to defuse another nasty surprise. *All in a day's work*, Slade thought

FIFTY

Assistant Director of FSB

Dr. Boris Andreev placed a call to agent in charge Damien Petrov. Petrov picked up on the second ring. "Petrov here," Damien said. "Oh, it's you, sir."

"How is the investigation going?" Dr. Andreev inquired. Dr. Andreev got involved when finding out that the stolen car belonged to Dr. Maxim Lenin, the foremost quantum scientist in Russia. He immediately alerted all Military districts in Russia to be on the lookout for these people. Boris didn't give them much to go on except a general description. Like himself, they were a little surprise on the lack of information. However, he did inform them that the three were heading to Severodvinsk; no doubt to one of the nuclear submarine shipyards to gather information about the latest design of their nuclear subs. On the conference call he told them that they needed to be ready for them either at the train station or at the various security checkpoints surrounding the city. It wouldn't be long until all three of them would be in their clutches.

Lev Ivanov, special agent in charge for the Northern Military District thought for a moment and then addressed the assistant director. "Sir, exactly how are we going to catch them with such sketchy information?"

"With irritation in his voice, he thundered, "we have their train tickets that show their names and visas and we already have a pretty good description of them." "But…but" Let me finish Lev." Even if they show different passports we'll still have the original passport numbers on the vouchers, and as I said their descriptions. No, they'll be ours. Now, if there aren't any more questions, let's get these guys. The line went dead.

Dr. Andreev sat back in his chair and folded his hands in a tent and thought all the years he fought his way through the ranks to get where he was today. It wasn't easy dodging all the political land mines, and if this is important that he thinks it is and if the culprits are found and at least sent to Siberia; the Directorship would be his.

FIFTY-ONE

Severodvinsk

After checking the deposit box at the train station and leaving the tickets to St. Petersburg there. They took their special permits with them, got their new passports that matched their new physical descriptions, and had one more thing to do before leaving. Gary already had a Russian quilted hat on his head when he reached in and got the mossy brown wig and headed to the nearest men's bathroom (tualet) and after Gary came out wearing his quilted hat, over his wig they were ready to go. They hopped a trolley and went to the nearest check point, in order to enter the interior part of the city. Gary showed the three special passes and identification credentials to the guard standing at his post. The guard asked Gary to pull back his hat so he could see his hair. The guard then told him he looked like a girl and all four of them laughed at Gary's expense. *Anything for the cause,* Gary thought. After the inspection of their special permits, credentials and their backpacks they were allowed through. *Good old Russia*, Jake thought, and thank God for Yuri delivering their equipment to the old industrial junk yard, including the C4. Otherwise, they would have never gotten through carrying their additional equipment and explosives. They hopped on another trolley heading to the northeast section of the city. As they traveled to their destination, Jake was looking for a good candidate to pilfer. Going around one of the submarine bases, Jake spotted a perfect suspect parked at one of the parking lots. They got off at the next stop nearest the vehicle and walked back the short distance to an older KamAZ. Jake casually tried the driver door and it opened. All three looked around and found no one nearby so they got in. While the other two looked around Jake got into his small tool box hidden in his right boot and took a two piece ceramic flat blade screwdriver out and split the steering column to get to the ignition wires. He cut the exposed wires and touched the copper leads together and voila! the engine stuttered alive. They were in business for the next part.

They drove to the industrial park near the silo and collected the rest of their gear, compliments of Yuri.

"Boy I don't know how he does this?" Jake said, looking at Gary.

"He has friends," Gary remarked, and before Jake could say anymore, continued. "I don't know all of his friends and I really hope the ones that are helping him on this caper are reliable."

"Oh good God!" Jake huffed. "We are not playing keystone cops here. This is a top secret military operation here."

"Gotcha," Gary said. "Of course everything has been run through your boss and everyone that is helping us has been checked by the CIA. You know this, Jake."

Slade looked at his partner with concern in his steely black eyes, and said," hey you okay buddy? You look a little jumpy."

"Ya, I'm okay, just a little edgy. I'm a little worried about Zoey and what she is going through."

"What's that?" Slade asked, showing more concern in his black eyes.

"I'll talk to you about it later. Right now let's concentrate on our plan"

Larceny was in the wind as they traveled to their next destination. They parked the old truck as best they could out of site a short distance from the complex. Jake checked the schematics before getting out and everything looked as it should. They checked the Geiger for a base reading and it was not quite as high as the reading at Yerma, but high enough for concern. There wasn't any cyclone fence around the installation per se, but a low concrete berm with a metal gate for entrance. The lock looked hefty compared to the one in Yerma, and his bolt cutters wouldn't do the trick. He lit the oxygen-acetylene torch and cut his way through. This place looked clean and tidy compared to Yerma and Jake could tell the maintenance was done on a regular schedule. They moved to the silo door, and Jake had to use his torch again to burn through the lock. As they went in and down the corrugated piping he could see the place was clean and organized. "I want to get out of here fast, so let's make short work of this place." Luckily he found an maintenance schedule taped to one of the control room's walls. Gary looked at it and said they were good for another of couple of weeks.

While Jake and Slade were checking around the control desk and its underside for any devices that could dampen their progress, Gary was checking the area for any trip wires, and infrared lasers with a can of smoke. Nothing was found around the control desk and the general area of the room. No I.E.Ds either. They didn't want to be blown to smithereens. Gary was now using his specialized equipment to see if there was a back door to the control launch system–he was curious. There wasn't so now it was time to act like meth heads again. Jake used the portable torch system to cut each end off. This took some time, and while Jake was cutting Gary and Slade were holding visquene around the cutting area to reduce the exposure of sparks to the inside of the control room. Even though all three of them check every square inch of the floor, surrounding walls, the corrugated tubing and even the ceiling for infra-red lasers and trip wires, they were now sure there wasn't anything else including I.E.Ds that could be set off. They worked quickly and efficiently and again, used a bucket and snow to cool the cut brass ends faster. They wanted out of there as soon as possible.

They could tell on their way out to the site that the town was very busy. In addition to three submarine development locations there was an automobile manufacture, couple of heavy equipment places, two auto dealerships and all kinds of businesses. Everyone seemed very busy– the place was a going concern. This helped the three tourists to remain completely anonymous. There special passes were cleared for them to observe one of the submarine development companies. But who really cared because of all the work that was going on.

After the ends cooled they lugged the launch control unit pieces to the flatbed and tied them down. *So far, so good,* Jake was thinking when all of a sudden they heard a blast and Jake abruptly stopped the truck. They looked around and finally got out and discovered the truck's right front tire blew out. Slade stepped up to the truck's tool box while Jake searched under the truck for a spare. There wasn't any. So they drove the truck the remaining half mile to the industrial junk yard with sparks a flying like a spinning wheel. They really had no other choice. After unloading the cargo and disarming the C4 and finding an old shovel they buried the broken chunks of it deep in the ground in separate places around the site and hid everything else amongst the old industrial equipment. They started walking back to town while Jake got on his sat phone and called, James.

He picked it up on the second ring. "Ya what's going on, Jake?" His boss asked.

" We're sort of in a pickle," Jake said as he rubbed a hand through his wavy blond hair.

"Is your encryption on?" the Deputy Secretary asked, before going further.

"Of course it is." Jake knew his boss well. James was a retired colonel in the army like his old boss, David Peterson. They were both made of gunfire and starch and took no flak from most anyone. Unlike his former boss, James was a diehard bachelor. Little in stature, but big on smarts and hardly ever went into preamble when initiating or receiving a call.

"We are mostly done with the operation here, when one of the truck's tires blew out, and there is no spare. We improvised and stole an old KamAZ on our way here to save us some time." Jake went on and told his boss the rest of the story.

"We only have a couple of hours left, sir, before our train leaves for St. Petersburg and we'll never make it on time walking on foot. Can you send a car to collect us?"

"In the time slot we have and the security being as tight as it is, I don't think so. You're on your own and you'll have to steal another car and get yourselves there on time.

This is what happens when you don't follow protocol, and don't tell me, "But sir.". "We'll talk about this when you get back." The line went dead.

"We're by ourselves until we get to the train station." Jake said. He knew the schedule was squeezing them, plus they still had to go through security with their special permits, in order to leave the zone right before arriving to the train depot. They didn't take the city's trolley layout and schedules with them so they really had to steal another vehicle to make it work.

James leaned his short-wiry frame back in his chair and wondered what in tarnations happened to Jake. He was always flawless in following protocol. This time, he went out on a limb and put not only his group in danger but also the underpinnings of the agency. He would have to have a heart-to-heart conversation with the big fella when he got…that's if he got back.

FIFTY-TWO

Time is Golden

After walking a couple miles and getting colder by the minute, Jake spotted a Ford Sollers on the outskirts of the city. The car was a joint venture between Ford and Russia. This one was white and looked quite new and in good shape. It was a four door sedan and larger than the Lada. The silo and the industrial junk park were far away from the city because of possible radiation leakage. Jake got his tool kit out of his backpack and found his handy slim-jim. Luckily the inspection missed it the first time when they had their special permits and credentials checked. This time he would discard anything that would even remotely alarm the Russian authorities before going through the security zone, right before arriving at the train station.

Jake handed Slade the city map while he and Gary looked on as Jake made short work of stealing the car. The newer Ford Sollers even had a GPS system so Slade plugged in the address, in Russian, to the security point they needed to go through. They had to hurry to honor the time stamp on the permit. *Once again*, Jake thought, *Russia was still suffering from the cold war syndrome.* They would ditch the car and dispose of the offending tools a mile or so from the security zone and hop a trolley to go the rest of the way. They needed to look like tourists for sure to get past the check point. Once through, the train station was only a short block away.

"Good thing the truck was a junker," Slade said, as Jake was driving to their destination.

"Why's that?" Gary asked, with a perplexed look on his narrow face.

"The truck will fit in nicely with all the other junk scattered around the yard." Slade said.

"Good point," Gary responded. "We wouldn't want to make it too easy for the Russian authorities."

"That's for sure," Jake pealed in. "We sure as heck don't want to take the visitation tour of the Russian gulags, or worse." Everyone nodded at his remarks. "Okay guys, heads up, we're getting close to ditching the car. Look over there," Jake pointed at a vacant lot with a lot of blackberry briars and tall weeds. "I bet the Russians dispose their old refrigerators and water heaters in there. I know I would." After he discarded the tools deep into the briar patch, their next stop was the car's turn. They continued on their way until Jake found a spot to do away with the vehicle close to a trolley stop. He looked at the time and they only had an hour left to get to the train station, and he was hoping the inspection process wouldn't take too long. They were cutting it close.

They got off the trolley pretending to joke and laugh in Russian as they approached the security post. Once again, Gary took the lead and spoke to the guard in Russian while handing over the special permits. They didn't need them anymore. While the guard was checking their credentials and the contents in their knapsacks they stood around and joked and laugh waiting for the process to finish. Afterward, they thanked the guard and proceeded to the train depot.

FIFTY-THREE

Train Depot

After arriving at the train depot, and Gary discarding his wig they collected their tickets from the deposit box and their luggage from the baggage room and checked in at the counter. After train security went through their belongings they received their carriage CB passes to St. Petersburg. They took their seats in the vestibule and waited.

Jake thought back about disarming the SS-19 in Severodvinsk. It was too easy. They didn't even have to create a distraction, and this bothered him greatly. Sure they had an unexpected surprise with a flat tire. *So what!* He thought. He had a distinct feeling that something was going to happen somewhere down the line. He could feel it. He couldn't see anywhere where they were being followed, but those sneaky Russians had their ways. One chasing ghosts was more than enough, let alone all three doing it. Jake knew they were high on the wanted list and he was on high alert and very cautious. He wasn't going to say anything to Slade and Gary yet. Why bother them! Going forward he would be on triple alert, and he knew how important this operation was. I mean taking down Russia's nuclear capabilities was no easy or small task. *On this they needed luck besides skill,* he thought.

Ten minutes later their train arrived. There was no waiting getting on to their carriages. Once again they had different carriage cars. There was no alternate trains like the long trip from Yerma to Severodvinsk. This was a 25 hour trip going mainly south from the White Sea. Once there, the real work would begin in earnest. Taking down Russia's nuclear capabilities was a tall order.. It would involve two main phases, land and sea going and it would be slightly staggered. Gary knew it would be a tricky operation, especially on the sea- going side, but they had the technology to pull it off. The big question was did they have the skills to utilize the technology. Jake knew that Gary was brilliant, but was he efficient. It wouldn't be long until he found out. Heaven help them if it there was a snafu, or the technology didn't work as designed or touted. If so, a Russian gulag in Siberia had their names scripted in brass on it. Of course, there was always the gallows to look forward to. The Russkies were very inventive when it came to torture and pain.

FIFTY-FOUR

FSB

Dr. Boris Andreev, paced back and forth with his hands folded behind him in his large corner office on the fourth floor of the Kremlin building waiting for more useful information. It has been a couple of days since anything has come in and he was getting nervous. Suddenly his assistant came barreling into his office to have him pick up on line 4. Damien Petrov was waiting.

"Yes, Damien, what do we have?" the assistant director said, waiting impatiently.

"It's not very good, sir."

"What do you mean?" Dr. Andreev thought, *you baboon.*

"We checked all the security points around Severodvinsk and no substantial evidence was found that the three people we are looking for were detained." Petrov said, with a tremor in his voice. Normally, he was very self-confident, but when speaking with the assistant director, he knew he had to tread lightly.

"Are you sure?" the assistant director said, with a dark message emanating from his voice.

"Sir, we checked thoroughly and no one came through remotely resembling their general appearance and or their names."

The assistant director thought for a moment and said, "Were there any groups of three men that came through any of the checkpoint?" He questioned.

"Let me check all of the scheduled information at all security checkpoints and I will get back to you shortly," Petrov quivered.

"You better, or you know what will happen!" Dr. Andreev huffed. The line went dead.

FIFTY-FIVE

The Trip

Once aboard and their luggage stowed, Slade and Gary met in Jake's cabin to review and study some of the pieces of the operation they were somewhat unfamiliar with. It wasn't Gary, but Jake and Slade that needed more primer. The sea going segment was vexing with so many places on the seabed were c-lines were installed. Actually, they all needed more review on this. If any of the Russian Akula and Yasen class attack submarines escaped detection and the virus didn't enter their communication lines to disarm them, the West would pay holy-hell for it and lose millions of civilians in their cities. Because there wasn't a defense bubble built yet, like the Iron Dome that we helped develop and build for Israel. They already knew some of their nuclear armament and as said nothing but the word devastating destruction came to mind. They still needed to study more on the nuclear armament and reactors. This was critical to the mission. The trio had to be dead on where and when to release the Stuxnet II virus. They also needed more study on all the communication systems that the Russians had on land and sea going.

On land they again had to looked at all the possibilities, but at a deeper level. There were a host of technologies with the most common called Land Mobile Radio system (LMR) which is a two way radio network used for first responders, such as police, fire and medical services. They often use dedicate frequencies and infrastructures to communicate on. LMR typically use portable radios, radios installed in vehicles, base stations for network control and repeaters to extend signal range. Another common communication system was cellular matrix. Today it is widespread and used for voice and data transmissions. Satellite conveyance provides connectivity to remote areas. Also county, state and federal authorities rely on the transmission accuracy and fluidity. Global Position Systems (GPS) are a part of land communication. Originally from Navstar GPS satellite based radio navigation system, and is now owned and operated by the United States Space Force agency. Like repeater stations for LMR signal extension, satellite transmissions can go from satellite to satellite to increase their range. Elon Musk's satellite internet uses thousands of satellites in low Earth orbit to transmit signals and provide high-speed broadband internet. It was used for communication in Western North Carolina. It's called Starlink and uses ground stations connected to fiber-optic networks, with satellite antennas tied to buildings or portable devices. There are six GPS systems, four owned by the United States, one by Japan and the other by India. Microwave transmission is for long-distance channeling data.

Jake and Slade knew a lot about land communication technology, but wanted to hone their skills to be sure. "Gary, I would like to divest here since you mentioned Elon Musk's name. I know Elon and Vivek Ramaswamy were asked by Trump to form a new advisory group that is comprised of very wealthy and savvy individuals. The advisory group is the Department of Government Efficiency (DOGE) and they are mandated to cut two trillion from the six plus trillion budget that Congress is working with. There are a host of eye-popping expenditures such as 1 million for race obsessed green group, or how about another million for a well-heeled LGBT group. I could go on and fill this book with pork Congress is spending on. I also understand now that Vivek is leaving DOGE and making a run for governor of Ohio. I wish him all the luck on that." But now it's my turn," Gary said. "Getting back to what I was talking about. I know, Frank Mulligan, is really worried about the United States debt. It's currently at 36 trillion and growing. You could create a bridge to the moon with the bills. plus we are paying more than one trillion to service the debt.

"What are we going to do about this?" Slade asked with a worried look on his face.

"I don't know. With everything going on including the immigration issues, Trump has his hands full, and he only has four years to correct many of the issues and get the country back on course. And I'm only talking about domestic issues and not international. Speaking of which, I'm really concerned about Iran. All the sanctions slowing down Iran's nuclear program expired in October of 2023, and as you know the Biden Administration hasn't done anything about it. Just dumb and lazy!" Gary exclaimed.

Jake stepped up and responded with "World War III here we come"

FIFTY-SIX

Russian Nuclear Submarines

Gary took a long moment to get control of his emotions after his outburst of what he thought were some of the problems of the United States. "Okay guys let's take a closer look at what kind of Russian nuclear subs we will be disarming. Fortunately, we only have to find and deal with 25 nuclear submarines. Five are in dry dock and are currently being decommissioned. This means their nuclear reactor and armament will be removed, and hence become toothless.

The first class is the Akula. By the way, as I said, akula in Russian means shark, and that they are. They were developed in the 80s and consequently updated throughout the years, and now we are dealing with the Akula II and Akula III. Even though the Russian Navy will start removing them from their fleet, nevertheless they are very deadly. They're pretty quick with 32 to 40 mph submerged. On the surface they are much slower with 12 to 20 mph. Their endurance is 100 days and an operating depth of 2,000 feet.

Now the important part. We will look at their armament. This is what we are stopping."

"What about their size?" Slade questioned.

"Who cares," Gary remarked. Were more concerned about what kind of damage they can cause. They have 4x533 mm torpedo tubes that handle 28 of those devils. Plus another 4x650 mm torpedo tubs that can fire 12 more torpedoes. Also, 1 to 3 Igla-M surface to air missiles. They are basically for surface detonations.

Communications on the surface are through Chiblis Surface Search radar, Medvyeditsa-945 Navigation system, and Molniya-M Satellite communications with MGK-80. Clearly they have redundant navigation systems to receive a host of different communications depending where they are at on the surface.

Under water communications are handled through Tsunami, Kiparis, Anis, Sintez and Kora Communications antennas. Also they have Paravan Towed VLF Antenna and Vspletsk Combat direction systems. These systems respond to different underwater cables, emitting commands, laid in the seabed. The Gepard, I believe is the last of the Acula III class and is the most advanced Russian submarine before the submarines of the Severodvinsk and Borei class were commissioned. Although the information I have is pretty sparse because of their secrecy, but nonetheless very important to our operation.

Another pick from Moscow, the Project 885 Yasen is actually the latest addition to the Russian fleet of nuclear-powered attack submarines. Their purpose in the Russian Navy is to replace the Akula class, which is also a powerful family of submarines.

The latest class of Russian nuclear submarines is pattern after the Yasen-M design and the first Yasen classes were commissioned in 2021 and six more are under construction. Based on the Akula class and Alfa class designs, the Yasen class is projected to replace the Russian Navy's current Soviet-era nuclear attack submarines. The Akula class is optimized for a hunter-killer role, whereas the Yasen class concept uses the platform as a nuclear guided missile submarine.

Yasen-class submarines are the first to be equipped with a fourth-generation nuclear reactor.[43][44] The reactor, built by Afrikantov OKBM,[45][46] will allegedly have a 25-30-year core life and will not have to be refueled. The main concern of nuclear submarines is how quiet they move submerged. The Russian sub, Kazan, wasn't detected for weeks submerged in the Atlantic a few years ago. This is, of course, grave concern to the U.S. navy."

You have to be kidding," Jake said, while shaking his head. "Is Russia's nuclear submarine technology superior to ours?"

Gary thought for a while before answering. "No it isn't, but it is close to the technology of the United States Sea Wolf class. You have to realize there has always been a race for the best technology between Russia and the U.S. for decades and even though the cold war has ended this is still ongoing. In fact the competition between the two countries is about most anything and his heating up. Think Sputnik."

I suppose so," Jake answered. "With our training Slade and I knew about the cold war, the Berlin Wall and other obstacles that our country took down from Russia, but I didn't quite know the extent of it and how severe the competition had become."

"Oh, yeah," Gary said, rubbing his hands together. "Now, let's take a look at their armament. The Yasen-class can launch long-range cruise missiles with nuclear or conventional warheads, up to 3,100 miles away. The submarine can carry 24 Oniks or 32 caliber cruise missiles, which are stored in eight or ten vertical launchers. They have ten 533 mm torpedo tubes armed with UGST-M heavyweight guided torpedoes. They also carry mines. They can carry anti-ship missiles and also anti-submarine missiles such as the RPK-7. Moreover, this is very important, these subs can carry the 3M22 Zircon hypersonic cruise missile, which can reach a top speed of Mach 9.0. And yes, they have now missiles similar to our Trident II D5 LE that can be launched under water. Finally, we are only looking at the two major classes of nuclear submarines that Russia has. They still may have a few outdated subs roaming around, but I highly doubt it."

"Gary, why are we studying this so intently? Jake asked.

"Fellas, we need to know what we're dealing with if we fail. I know this is a whole lot of pressure, but to be honest we need this. For all I know they may even strike Israel. Even if we miss one, that's death to millions of people!"

FIFTY-SEVEN

Trouble Abounds

Gary thought for a long while before going on with the plan. "Hey fellas if you don't mind I'm going to divest to answer a biting concern of mine."

"Where are you going with this?" His two friends asked.

"Well some people might not like what I am going to say, but it needs to be said. There are too many people in your country that have their eyes off the ball for one reason or another. I personally believe that President Biden and his administration has ruined your country like no other, and it only took four short years to do it. And your country was already on its way. Congress's annual budget–spending in 2019 was 4.4 trillion. Now its 7.3 trillion per year, and your total debt is over 36 trillion. The interest to service the debt is over one trillion per year. Your Administration and Congress are out of control and discretionary spending is at an all-time high. How are your children and grandchildren going to get out of this without austere measures taking place? Your homeland security has been diminished to the level that it doesn't even look like there is any surety at all. I mean your safety has been pushed back decades. And as you know, that's the tip of the problem. I mean your borders both North and South are mired in geo-politics because of the immigration problems. I'm discussing this because of the events that have occurred."

"Are you thinking about the terror attack on New Orleans and Las Vegas?" Jake responded shaking his head.

"Yes, I guess you could say that's the catalyst for my outburst for the way the United States is acting. Let's stay on this for a moment. Biden is so out of touch that shortly after the attacks happened he went on your cable networks to say we should be more worried about white supremacy than ISIS terrorism. Are you kidding!" Gary roared.

Slade looked at Jake with a wide eyed expression and said, "I've never seen Gary so animated."

"Me neither."

Gary looked at his friends and continued. Your mid-size and large cities will become military zones."

"What do mean?" Slade responded.

"Okay," Gary said while he was getting his second wind. "Your avenues and streets will have to be barricaded with bollards to keep vehicles from driving on the sidewalks killing pedestrians. You will have shot spotters everywhere. Military drones in the sky will be patrolling your streets and some will have weapons. Your schools will be hardened to the point that students will not leave under any circumstances without their parents being there. "

"You have to be kidding," the soldiers said with horror written across their faces.

"Sorry, but this is what I see and the world sees this too, because everything will change."

"But if I'm correct, you are talking about a dystopian society," Jake said with grave concern in his blue eyes.

"Ya, you will still have freedom, but it will be sorely restricted and come at great costs. You don't even know what your government is doing, because it's so opaque. What about all those drones? Have they said anything about them. No, they haven't–there's no transparency anymore. Can you think back when you were kids."

"Now wait a minute, Gary. You're not going off the rails, are you?" Jake said as he looked Gary squarely in his eyes.

"Of course not. I have some friends that lived in Portland, Oregon years ago. When their sons were about 10 to 12 years old, they went downtown all the time on trolleys all by themselves. Sure Portland was only 300,000 to 400,000 back then, but the point is they could go almost anywhere without any problems. Today, you can barely let your children out of the front door without being afraid that something will happen to them."

"I think you're correct," Slade answered. "I know the number of helicopter parents are increasing as problems grow. Even though my daughters, Marla and Darla are in their twenties I worry about them all the time. The chances of something happening to them are expanding as time goes on."

"Boy, I'm sure glad I don't have any kids," Jake answered. "Heck, I'm not even married."

"Well buddy, I'm sure your time will come," Slade responded with a sly look on his face.

"Getting back to your public schools. A lot of them are cesspools of chaos. How can students learn in this kind of environment? Also, your government didn't handle covet-19 well when it struck. They locked down everything and now you practically have a lost generation of kids. Heck, ever since the covet-19 dilemma, federal workers still haven't come back to work. I hear their unions want another five years for their workers to work from home. What about all those federal buildings that remain empty, who's going to pay for the maintenance and repairs of all those buildings. Can you say 'taxpayers'. In addition, a lot of your children are now being radicalized by your liberal college professors. There are demonstrations everywhere – Anti-Semitism, and Hamas is growing more powerful by the year. Many in your society doesn't know what Hamas means, including your college kids. To clarify, it is the Islamic Resistance Movement abbreviated Hamas and is a Palestinian nationalist Sunni Islamist political organization with a military wing called Izz al-Din al-Qassam Brigades. It has governed the Israeli-occupied Gaza Strip since 2007. The Palestinian people are great, but the military wing worries me."

"Ya we know far more about this than the ordinary citizen," Jake said in earnest.

"Now let me finish my diatribe!," Gary huffed. "Instead of teaching STEM they're instructing various ideologies. High School students now think US History is pulp fiction. You ought to see what Frank Mulligan has to say about this! In the early sixties your education system was number one in the world, now the number is forty–last place. And I'm sure if the range was longer the US would still be in last place. The cost per student is in first place.

Like Frank Mulligan said, the US was in first place in the early sixties. President Jimmy Carter was really a decent person and this was proven over and over again since he left his Presidency. But being President wasn't his strong suit. After leaving office, his prime project was Habitat for Humanity, and it was and is still a striking example of how people when working together can accomplish great things. However, when he created the Department of Education in the mid-seventies this was his fall from grace. Before then the states controlled and educated their students and were doing quite will. But when the Federal Government stepped in and took control and centralized the operation, it failed miserably. Of course, there is Iran and inflation, but we won't go there. Just ask Frank Mulligan in Path To Peril.

FIFTY-EIGHT

Sea Going Russian Nuclear Sub Communications

"**G**ary thought for a long time to get under his legs again. He had to quit thinking about the United States current situation, and continue to ponder the operation. He looked over the schematics on the table for a long moment before he began. "Russian nuclear submarines primarily use acoustic signals to communicate while submerged at sea, utilizing underwater loudspeakers and hydrophones to transmit messages over long distances, often through dedicated seabed communication lines (systems). They are placed in strategic locations by the Russian Navy, similar to the US SOSUS system. This method is known as "sonar communication" and is the most reliable way to contact submarines deep underwater."

"What's the heart of the matter here?" Slade questioned looking at Gary with deep concentration in his dark brown eyes.

"There are a couple of things here," Gary said thinking about how to answer this. First, the trick is locating all the Russian embedded c-lines on the ocean floor. Second, this will lead to locating all the Russian Navy command centers that use these lines to communicate with their subs."

"How are we going to do this?" Slade asked. He was now looking at Jake and the only reaction he got from his friend was shrugged shoulders.

"Well, do you guys remember us discussing the internet map of the world. The one that is always growing and contains all the Internet Provider Services. From these IPS we can get the physical addresses to all of their locations, including the ones in Russia. This will help us to double check the IPS through their c-lines' locations."

"We can!" Jake exclaimed with a surprise look on his face.

"Oh ya, and much more," Gary answered back. "We can also get their surrounding locations like Google Earth, and this is where you guys come in. According to the most current information I have, the Russian Navy primarily communicates with its submarines through a network of command centers, with the main headquarters located in Moscow, and the Sevastopol in Crimea that controls all sub traffic on the Black Sea. Finally a secondary command bunker at Gorki-25 which these centers can issue orders to the submarine fleet.. This utilizes various communication methods including VLF transmitters, satellite communications, and airborne relays. Actually the Gorky-25 refers to a ship, specifically the "Maxim Gorky" class cruiser, which is a highly updated Soviet warship; therefore, its location would depend on where the specific "Gorky-25" vessel is currently docked or stationed. Generally, it would be within the waters of Russia as this is the primary operating area for this class of cruiser. The Maxim Gorky comes from a long line of cruisers dating back to at least World War I. So we have the main Russian Navy communication centers located on land in Moscow, and a moving and portable command center, Gorky-25 at sea, except when it is dry-docked for maintenance. Our job is to find out which Russian Navy command center we can infiltrate and have an unsuspecting Russian officer or scientist insert Stuxnet II virus for us. Another method is for us to insert it ourselves. However its paramount that nobody knows, in order to successfully complete the next to the last phase of the operation."

"I have been thinking how sensitive and important this operation is," Jake responded with a heavy hand. "But how does this tie in to the Iran action."

"It is imperative that the Iran situation is started and completed at least a few months after this plan. Of course this depends on how close they are in producing a fission bomb. If this is the case, I'm sure my country will take care of this before Iran can fire any atomic weapons. Remember, in addition of them producing a nuclear bomb, Iran also has to learn the technology for incorporating the device atop a missile."

"Isn't North Korea helping them in this area?" Slade asked in his normal gravelly voice.

"They sure are," Gary quipped. "We have to keep a close eye on this along with any Chinese developments."

"What a complicated and screwed up world we live in," Jake replied, shaking his head.

"We sure are," Gary responded. Now getting back to Russian Navel communications, I have some good news." Before anyone interrupted he continued. "Of course you already know we're heading to Saint Petersburg for a variety of reasons, but foremost is to visit the, Maxim Gorky dry-docked at the Admiralty Shipyards. It will be there for another three month for maintenance and repairs. How lucky can we be!" Gary yelped.

Jake looked at Gary and Slade and reminded them of the dangers of the operation. "Guys we have received two lucky breaks, probably three."

"What do you mean?" Gary asked, looking around the small cabin.

"We got that old Mercedes-Benz to get us out of MSU and even though we got a flat tire on that old truck everything else went smoothly. We didn't even need to create a distraction. You do know we got through the security zone in Severodvinsk carrying some items in our backpacks that could've raised suspicion and possibly detained us. Fellas our plans have worked, but we've have been too lucky. Man, I can feel it in my bones that something is coming, and coming hard. And, ya I know I've already said this before."

All of a sudden gloom and doom played its role in the room. "Boy, you sure know how to wreck a good afternoon," Gary said.

"He's right," Slade responded, looking at his friend. "There's too many things that can scramble the operation, so we need to be on our best."

Gary looked at his two friends and said, "I suppose your right. I think I was getting a little ahead of myself."

All three fell into deep thought wondering if anything could hit them. For sure they all need to be careful, lest they become residents in the Siberian gulags or worse.

FIFTY-NINE

Afternoon Trip

After the afternoon meeting in Jake's cabin, Gary excused himself and went to his cabin for a mid-day snooze. He was tired and he knew why. Before leaving Israel and being invited to the Department of Homeland Security (DHS) in the United States he went to an oncologist recommended by his regular physician and discovered that he had a somewhat aggressive cancer of his prostate. Dr. Benjamin Ezra recommended that he take radiation treatments to slow the growth and eventually shrink the size. At that point, Gary could decide what he wanted to do. He could do surgery, more radiation to control the growth, or look for advanced medication such as Orgovxy. This medication lowers the patient's testosterone levels, keeps the Gleason numbers low and thus controls the cancer's growth. In many cases patients die with it not from it. He was already in his mid-fifties, a small man with an ever increasing hunched back, bespectacled and nearly bald. Physically, he was the opposite of his counterparts. Jake and Slade were tall and muscular, both forty and years of military training. They were great, but Gary was the brains of the operation.

After leaving Gary for his nap, Jake and Slade went to the observation deck with 360 degree windows. They sat down on the cushy seats and both ordered soft drinks.

"Look at this gorgeous view isn't it just wonderful," Slade said. "Some of it looks like Talga"

Looking at the countryside himself, Jake answered, "What's that."

"Where we can see between areas of snow it's a mixture of swamps with a forest of birch, pine and spruce and it covers the north, east and center of the oblast."

"How do you know all of this?" Jake replied while receiving their soft drinks from the Porter.

Slade took a long pull of his soft drink, looked at his friend, and said, "remember I'm part Russian so naturally I'm curious about my homeland and have done a little research on it throughout my years of military training. You knew that."

"I guess so," Jake said taking another sip of his cola.

"Ya, Russia is considered the largest country in the world covering vast area across two continents, Europe and Asia."

"Okay I knew that. But also I'm still troubled about how smoothly things are going. Buddy, you're aware on other assignments we have had, at times, where we have run into road blocks."

"Ya, I know, but we have to deal with them when they come. We have to be prepared and as our boss says, anticipate–be proactive."

"That's for sure," Jake answered.

About then, Gary found them after his siesta. "I'm hungry, you guys ready for dinner in that beautiful dining car."

After a sumptuous dinner they all met again in Jake's room for further discussions.

SIXTY

Lev Ivanov (FSB)

The special agent in charge for the Northern District, Lev Ivanov, was as baffled as the next person until he received news that three males had vouchers for Saint Petersburg from Severodvinsk. That in itself didn't bring up any flags, but when he found that the voucher's numbers were consecutive that told him in all likelihood that they knew each other. The odds were in their favor that they had found the right people. They still only had a general description of the three, but Lev went with his haunch and made arrangements to have them followed and detained for questioning.

The assistant director was breathing down his neck and wanted answers. He knew the Moscow train station at Vosstaniya Square was huge and the time of day at 9am wasn't in the best interests in capturing the three, but they had to try. They might have found information on Quantum Mechanics and AI at one of the Science and Technology buildings at Moscow State University (MSU). They were chased and broke through a barricade set up at the main entrance in an old 1985 Mercedes Benz sedan. That car belonged to Dr. Maxim Lenin a foremost scientist researching Quantum Mechanics and Computing. Who knows what information was in his car and what they stole from the building. He also stationed other members of his team around the station—just in case. *No, they had to be captured and soon,* he thought.

SIXTY-ONE

Land Base Communication Locations

Back in Jake's room each poured a cup of that wonderful espresso from the canister the porter left with them from the dining car.

"Oh, this is great stuff," Gary said, poring another cup.

"You better be careful or you'll have trouble sleeping tonight," Jake chuckled and went on. "We got bigger fish to fry then trying to research the ingredients of our espresso. Gary, do you try to delve into everything you come across."

"Pretty much. I guess that's because of my scholastic training and my curiosity of the great unknown. Okay, let's look at what we have, and he brought up two computer screens on the table.. One showing the internet map with all the digital connections of the world in real time. The other screen had the physical locations of the command centers that control and launch land based Intercontinental Ballistic Missiles (ICBMs) and hypersonic missiles. I believe everyone pretty much understands how this works, in other words their launch patterns for ICBMs. They go up to low space and then drop down to a another continent for their target. Some have MIRV warheads to spread a wider area of destruction. Their drawback is they are easy to track and possibly intercept and shoot down. To change course a bit, it wasn't until relatively recently that the Russians could fire long range missiles while submerged, and this also includes hypersonic missiles. Russia is pretty advanced in this technology and their missiles can reach Mach 13 around 9,000 mph."

"How do they actually work?" Slade interjected, rubbing the dark stubble on his face.

"Gary thought for a moment to mentally gather the information he needed, and began with, "Russian hypersonic missiles, like the "Kinzhal"

(Dagger), operate by being launched from an aircraft or a submerged submarine reaching high speeds using a rocket booster, then gliding at hypersonic speeds on a low trajectory towards their target, making them difficult to intercept due to their maneuverability and speed, often exceeding Mach 6 (six times the speed of sound), while flying close to the ground to evade radar detection; they can carry both conventional and nuclear warheads. The ones launched from land are larger and as I said before, can reach speeds of 9,000 mph because of larger rocket engines. Now another class launched from submerged submarines use scramjet engines and can reach speeds of Mach 7, maybe Mach 8 and then glide to their target. Their flight paths while gliding can also be changed. Their range is much shorter than the ICBMs, but nonetheless very lethal. I believe their rocket fired until they reach a speed of about Mach 4 or 5 and then the scramjet engines take over."

Jake thought a moment on this. He and Slade already knew the technology, but it would be nice to get a quick refresher, and he asked, "what do you mean by this?" Jake asked.

"Well, when an aircraft reaches a speed of around Mach 4 or 5 the friction caused by the incoming airflow is hot enough to ignite the hydrogen fuel kept on board that is used to propel the plane."

"But why hydrogen fuel instead of jet fuel?" Slade asked, searching for answers.

"You know that jet fuel is made of hydrocarbons and is much heavier than hydrogen, and has a slower ignition rate, among other things.

Let's do a little exercise here. You know that the SR-71 Blackbird was developed by the Skunkworks division at Lockheed Martin in the sixties."

"Ya, a lot of people know this," Slade said. "It was a top-secret program for decades and we only found out in the nineties what it's ceiling and top speed was."

"About 100,000 feet for ceiling and Mach 3.5 for speed. But did you know that it was only about 500 to 1,000 mph away from kicking in scramjet engines because of the heat created from the velocity and friction of the wind." Gary answered.

"No, I didn't know that."

"If they could have gotten to Mach 4 or 4.5 with conventional jet engines they would have had scramjet propulsion figured out. Instead, technology relied only on rocket engines back then. You know all about the studies on X15. Now since you know more about missiles in general, I need to divest from this subject and get back to the locations of the land based command centers that control these monsters. There are also two of them identical to the number of sea going command centers.

"One is in Moscow and the other is buried under the Urals at the Kosvinsky Mountain. The Russian Strategic Missile Troop (RSVN) command is a branch of the Russian Armed Forces that controls the country's land-based intercontinental ballistic missiles (ICBMs). The RVSN was founded in 1959 and was part of the Soviet Armed Forces until 1991. Now the Strategic Rocket Force (SRF) manage these missile systems. Like I said the one in Moscow is located in a suburb called Kuntsevo.

Okay the paramount question is: how do we enter the virus in to their systems. One, into their sea going system on the Gorky-25 dry docked at the Admiralty shipyards in Saint Petersburg.

Once again Yuri has come to our aid. Andrei Nickolov is a technician for the SRV and has been disenchanted with his homeland for years The Vladimir Putin Administration has not been kind to his family. They jailed his uncle, Albert Nickolov, and one of his nieces. His uncle is now in one of the gulags in Siberia. And this is for only complaining on how corrupt the Putin Administration is. The way I understand it, he is considered a political prisoner, and has been challenging Putin for years. In August, 2020 Albert really went off when Alexi Navalny was poisoned with a Novichok nerve agent. At that point, they tried Albert as a political scientist working against the State and jailed him, first in Moscow and later sent him to Siberia."

"What a bummer," Jake said, "but what happened to his niece?"

"That's even more sad. After her uncle was jailed, the Russian authorities began to follow, Anna Nickolov, because she was really close to Albert. The Federal Security Service (FSB) tracked her electronically on the internet as well as physically. The Service knew her better than herself and really did hound her from the shadows. They eventually found some evidence that she was in alliance with the opposing party against Putin, and a huge influencer on the internet. They didn't even bother with a phony trial and poisoned her with Thallium.

It's tasteless and odorless and is commonly used. It is very difficult to detect."

"Is Andrei a true patriot of the United States." Slade asked showing concern in his deep gravelly voice.

Gary thought for a long moment before answering. "Normally you guys would know more about this from DHS, but since Yuri is a close friend of mine I was asked to follow up on this with you guys. Andrei not only has been heavily investigated and tracked by your intelligent agencies, but also by Mossad. The guy is golden and will be our way in to the Strategic Rocket Force (SRF). We will in no way be directly involved with the transfer of the Stuxnet II except to give the thumb drive to him."

"Do we know how this will occur? Slade asked, wondering about all of this.

"In this case it is better we know nothing about this in case the Russian authorities pick us up for questioning."

"Fat chance in that happening," Jake answered. *He and Slade were always fully briefed on their operations before going out.* He thought. "Well isn't this ironic. I bet the Mossad had something to do with this. After all they're known as the best intelligence agency in the world, but it still eats at me not fully knowing every small detail of the operation. I mean if something does go wrong with this part of the plan, we will not know how to properly react to the situation."

"I would think so," Gary replied. "But your government wants it this way so we need to follow their line of thinking on this."

"Well I still don't like it," Jake intoned, looking at Slade.

"I'm with Jake on this," Slade said. "We have been in some pretty tight situations, but always found a way to maneuver out of them, because we knew every detail of the plan. You know the more I think about this the more I'm becoming suspicious. This seems almost crazy like they expect us to get captured by the Russian authorities." He looked at his friend, "maybe you need to call James and get this verified."

"Now wait minute," Gary implored. "I'm not leading you on guys. This is what I was given for instructions. I agree if there is a snafu we need to know about this."

Jake was already on his sat phone calling his boss. It was 7am Eastern time and James picked up the call on the first ring and without preamble said, "what's up, Jake. I wasn't expecting your call. Is everything okay, and is your scrambler on?"

"Ya, encryption is good," Jake said. "The crew and I have had a little discussion going on about a segment of our plan."

"Okay…" James said in a hesitant voice. "You guys in trouble or something?"

"No, nothing like that," Jake replied. "It has to do with the SRF technician, Andrei Nickolov. Is he to be trusted? And our we not to know what is going on with the hand off of the thumb drive to him.?" Jake questioned.

"You know that Mossad is part of this operation, right?" James said, becoming fully awake.

"I know that, sir, but can they be fully trusted? We don't want to be walking in to a trap."

"Our intelligent agencies and Mossad say he has been sorely disgusted with Russia for some time, especially after his uncle was jailed and his niece poisoned. Andrei wants to help us in any way he can."

"Okay, but why have we not been filled in on the particulars on the transfer of the Stuxnet II virus.?" Jake questioned.

"Jake, that was Mossad's call. They wanted to keep you out of the loop on this part in case you were captured or questioned by the authorities. Think about it. What more do you need to know about this except for the transfer of the thumb drive? What's the difference? From the transfer point on, it's all in the hands of Andrei," his boss shot back. "Just do your job and will talk when you get back." The line went dead.

Jake thought about this for a while before turning back to his friends and decided that everything is okay and we need to follow the plan explicitly. They got off the train the next morning in Saint Petersburg and as they collected their luggage from the porter, Jake saw an action from the corner of his eye that indicated danger. There were three big men dressed in dark attire motioning toward them.

SIXTY-TWO

The Chase

Jake casually turned to his friends and motioned that they were possibly being followed, and told them what they needed to do. They had one good thing going for them as they started heading toward the massive doors of the Moscow train station, located in the center of the city on Vosstaniya Square. The station was a wide building with an impressive facade, a clock tower, and a gold railway map on the western wall. The depot was as big as Grand Central in New York. It was 9am and the place was teeming with a huge crowd inside.

"Let's pick up the pace fellas," Slade said as he nonchalantly looked over his shoulder to check on the three strangers. Yup, they're following us and I'm sure they have other people inside the stationed to help corral us."

"Over my dead body," Jake said, miffed at the thought of being captured.

As they entered the huge depot through the massive turnstile doors on the east side of the station, the three friends split up to make it more difficult to follow them. Gary went toward one of the ticket counters and then suddenly veered to the right and headed to the west terminal doors. Because of his size he was hard to spot. That wasn't on his mind at the moment. What was on his mind was to follow the plan that Jake described. Then it happened. He was grabbed by one of the intruders and gruffly pushed in another direction. He could see that there was something in the man's hand that looked like a small hypodermic needle. *Oh no,* he thought. Just then Jake came up to the man from behind and brutally twisted the interloper's hand holding the needle. The invader received the needle in his neck and was invited to a near bench. Gary continued quickly to the west turnstile doors to meet a taxi that was a United States diplomatic vehicle. He hid amongst a large group of people waiting for their transportation. It wasn't long before the State car arrived and Jake and Slade were by his side. They jumped into the car and saw there were two occupants up front. Quick introductions were made and the big black Ford sped away. However, there was another black car chasing them at a high rate of speed and it wasn't long before gunfire erupted from the following vehicle. Luckily, the diplomatic auto was bullet proofed with polycarbonate, and the way it was accelerating it must have had a big V8 engine. They only had to go to the Crown Plaza hotel located 7 blocks away, but they needed to lose the other black car first. In the meantime, the front passenger was also firing at the auto chasing them. When the occupants of the following car realized that their hand guns were no match for the car in front of them they slowed down and turned right to a side street a mile into the chase, and Jake could see that the passenger on the front seat was already on his phone calling somebody. Just to be safe, Dave Cutting, the driver of the Diplomatic taxi continued to weave and turn in and out of traffic until they were safe from prying eyes before turning back to the hotel.

"Boy that was close,' Jake said to Dave, leaning toward the front seat.

"You guys must be important, because we really don't get that kind of reception around here. Actually, Saint Petersburg is a beautiful laid back city filled with tourists most of the time. We're heading toward Christmas now and the place will be jumping."

"Dave, you speak pretty good English and I guess you're not from around here" Jake asked.

No, I was born and raised in Manchester, England. After a good education I applied for the Diplomatic Corp, investigated, passed and was sent here. Been on the job three years here and I just love it."

"What about you, Gene?" Slade quizzed.

"Oh I was born in Georgia."

"Which one, the Georgia Republic or in the States." Gary chimed in Russian.

Can't you tell?'

"No, your Russian is so good, I would've ventured from the eastern bloc of Georgia."

"Ya all, I'm from Atlanta." Everyone chuckled.

"Well, you had me fooled, and I think my friends, too," as he looked around and saw them nodding their heads.

"I think we lost those bloody blokes now and I think we'll head back to the hotel. Besides, it's getting close to lunch and I bet you mates are getting hungry."

"Hungry or not can you drop us off at the service door? Don't want too much attention drawn to us."

"You're the boss Jake," Dave emphasized.

After the big Ford drove away, Jake slip his knife into the locked door and in a moment they hustled in and quickly walked down the service hall to get to the lobby. Jake carefully opened the entrance door to the lobby and looked around. It was clear, nothing out of place so they all came out and took their seats opposite to each other to get a better view on what was going on. Fifteen minutes later after reconnoitering the main floor,. they walked up one by one–covering the other and checked in. Again, different floors and different rooms. After they all got settled, Jake called them in to his room. Before going on to the next phase they were waiting for the call from Yuri that the thumb drive was transferred. Thirty minutes later, the call came in.

SIXTY-THREE

Federal Security Service (FSB)

"**N**o sir, we didn't lose them, but when we found that our handguns had no authority on their car, we turned off and called you." said Grigory Blum with a strange look on his face.

"Why did you do that?" Lev asked.

" What do you mean?" Grigory inquired, with a confused look on his face.

"How long have you been working for the service?"

"What does that have to do with anything?"

"I said how long?" Lev said raising his voice.

"Oh about fifteen years, sir." Grigory answered.

"You know you are a numskull, don't you?"

"What, look I've been here day and night, snow and rain and working my butt off for the agency and you're treating me like this?"

Lev thought a moment how he was going to frame his next response. "You should have discreetly followed them while requesting another car or two to cut them off. What were you thinking, or were you thinking?"

I guess you're right, sir." Grigory said, thinking about the possibility of abrupt retirement. The line went dead, and poor Grigory didn't know if he still had a job.

Lev now issued an all-points bulletin for his team to check all the hotels and motels in the area for recent check ins of single males. If there were any, he would have his agents beat feet there as soon as possible to gather more information. And if it was plausible, he would call backup. Now he would sit back and wait.

SIXTY-FOUR

Going To Admiralty Shipyards

Thinking back, Jake didn't need any of the devices they took with them to distract the authorities at Severodvinsk. He also got rid of the small amount–four chunks of C4 and the corresponding detonation devices in the same brushy area along with the other contents except for one small ceramic double edged knife and its sheaf–just in case. He mutilated the detonating devices before he scattered them in with the rest of the junk. He thought about leaving a small amount of explosives before deporting Severodvinsk and then stowing them in the train locker or somewhere in the depot and getting them later. *But why?* He thought. It would be far better to explode the devices then let the authorities find them later. No he would set them off remotely away from people to establish more confusion and danger. The confusion they're intending to create when Andrei inserts the other Stuxnet II thumb drive in the control system in Sevastopol in Crimea will be substantial. The control system monitors all sub traffic on the Black Sea and is manned by the Rocket Strategic Forces (RSF). Jake thought if another rather large explosion going off in Severodvinsk while they were on the Maxim Gorky; it would create more suspense and danger to the Russkies. Will let Yuri do the heavy lifting on this one. During the call from Yuri and with their scramblers on Jake told Yuri what he needed for distracting the shipyard authorities and especially the RSF on board. The RDX, detonators, det chords, if needed, and attack drones and their controls were to be left in an old tinted windowed van parked a block from the dock gates to the Maxim Gorky. In the two days before the attack, the trio studied the locale and especially the schematics of the Maxim Gorky intently day and night. Everything for the attack had to be in place and in the sequence and timed perfectly to cause the most panic, and appear that a group or squadron was attacking the ship.

"Yuri indicated yesterday that the virus had already been installed in the Moscow location and was ready to go," Jake indicated. "Now, we should be getting the van in the next few hours to help us complete this part of the operation, and God help us!

"We'll have to check the van thoroughly before we go," Slade replied while watching Jake nodding his head.

Jake thought for a moment. "Not only check it to make sure we have all the contents, but we'll have to set up everything in its proper order beforehand ready to fire. Because when it happens it will appear that all hell is breaking loose, and God please give us seven minutes to get in and out. Once on the bridge it will take Gary a minute or two to discover the designated USB port, on the control panel, to insert the thumb drive."

Gary chimed in and took the lead from Jake, because this was his area of expertise. "Once inserted it will only take 30 seconds for the quantum virus to break through the digital gateways and then calmly lay and wait for the GO command. It would take months, if not years, for a digital intrusion to break in of this nature. By then it wouldn't matter because the cipher, most likely based on prime numbers, would be changed on daily or weekly basis.

Once the GO command is initiated and staggered along with its brethren in Moscow, they will both start learning exactly where to go. Like a pack of vicious and hungry wolves looking for its prey, the virus like I already said, will break into sections, instruments if you will, and play the chords of an orchestra to increase the speed and the pathways of their learning curves as they go. They will smash through servers and mirrored servers, riding the routes instructed by their routers. Increasing their speeds, even more, they will also go through bridges and botnets, if there any, and go into the dark net still looking for any prey that might be lurking. Finally, the conductor will bring his batons down. Now the encore comes on as the virus backs out securing all botnets, if any, servers both physical and mirrored, routers, bridges, routes, flags and IPs and IPSs–everything. In other words where,what, why, who, when and how. Where do you begin? It is so daunting that most people will throw up their hands. Truly, only the most experienced, intelligent and gifted people can only begin to see and handle such a dilemma. Does this remind you of anything?"

"Sure does," Jake said nodding his head. "I need to call James again and report exactly where we're at along the spectrum. That's exactly what it is–a continuous line all the way to the end.

After the conversation with his boss, Jake turned to the others and said, "we are now at one of the most critical parts of Darkfall. James has given us the GO to execute this part of the plan. Fellas, the outcome of this phase of the plan could mean the difference between World War III and a more peaceful world.

SIXTY-FIVE

All Or Nothing

Early the next morning, Jake, Slade and Gary dressed in black and under cover of a moonless night stole an old Ford Soller, and drove it to the shipyards. They stopped at the SUV first to collect their equipment and don Russian Navy uniforms before going any further. Next they cut a small hole through the chain link fence for passage to the Maxim Gorky. They incapacitated the guard at the forward gangplank and moved silently up the walkway to the bow of the ship to stow C4 in the pigeon hold at the most forward point of the prow. They didn't want to do much damage except create a major distraction. The C4 would do its job because it contained 91 percent RDX which is a white crystalline solid easily mixed with other explosives to throw it's power around.

On the call with James it was also discussed that one of the drones could carry the package and drop it in the pigeon hold, especially since it was ready to be exploded by remote control instead of running a det cord. In the end it was decided for Jake and Slade would handle this. Even though the other way would bypass the guard stationed at the forward gangway entrance, it didn't matter. After Jake knock the soldier unconscious he used an anesthesia called MIT Propofol, commonly used by anesthesiologist for surgery. He had to be careful. He didn't want to kill the guy, but only keep him unconscious for a good long time–let's say 12 hours–perfect. Jake and Slade then went to the aft gangway and did the same thing.

Next they snuck back to the SUV to get the 40 drones ready to fly and to check on Gary to see if he was ready to go. He was!

"How did it go so far?" Gary whispered to Jake.

"Just like clockwork." Jake said, as he was checking the time. "Okay, we still need to arm the remaining few drones with mini explosives. These

AUVs will release little packets of surprise at various altitudes that will simulate tracer bullets exploding overhead.

Between the timed explosions at the bow and stern and tracer bullets flying overhead, the crew will be running around in panic mode wondering what hit them. And what will hit them is Gary Zimmerman, disguised as the ship's first officer, Boris Antonov. He'll give orders in Russian to anyone near him. He had studied him, speaks the same dialect and has a small frame like Boris–perfect for this phase of the operation. They entered the ships brow and with Jake and Slade dressed as junior officers flanking him, Gary gave terse orders to clear the way to the bridge. Amongst all the panic and confusion they swiftly entered the bridge. Jake and Slade stood at attention (guard) at the opening of the bridge while Gary went in to search the appropriate sections of the command center to insert the quantum thumb drive into the correct USB port. Once he inserted it, it only took about thirty seconds for the wolves to break through their flimsy digital gateways, like tearing flesh from its prey. Once there, Gary then retrieved the thumb drive and all three made their way back down the ship's brow, and gave orders to the guard to "carry on" as the three walked past him.

"Oh my God, I think we did it," Gary whispered, as they continued to walk away in plain sight.

When they arrived at the old SUV, they donned their uniforms over their normal clothes and tossed them into the SUV. As they walked another block to the stolen old Ford Soller, the SUV caught fire and was burning to the ground as they sped away to the Crown Plaza.

"God, that was amazing!" Gary bubbled.

"Don't say amazing to quickly," Slade said in his low gravelly voice. "We still have a long ways to go. Remember we're still in Russia far away from home and anything can still happen."

"Slade's right, Gary. We did an excellent job back there, but it won't be long before the authorities start piecing together the events that just transpired. Remember, the Federal

Security Service (FSB) similar to the old KGB is probably already looking into this. And they're going to be looking high and low and questioning anyone and everyone who could be associated with this. You have to remember they will be busy with the Mixim Gorky first. They'll take a close look at the damage to the ship and do forensics on the explosive and the type of drones that were used. Oh yes, they'll be crawling all over that boat until they're satisfied. And that's a big chunk of metal to be investigated. Plus we disabled the cameras before we entered the bridge and if I recall in the confusion no one saw us on the bridge. Of course they'll have to inspect the burnt out SUV one block away to see if there is any connection. Just the general site alone will take them days if not weeks to sift through all the evidence. We left them quite a mess. Plus, the explosions in Severodvinsk timed perfectly with the worm insertion on the Maxim Gorky. They'll have plenty to do as Jake was still running multiple scenarios through his mind when Slade spoke up." Of course there will be multiple teams of Russian agents scouring every bit of evidence that could be possibly linked to this incident. They will eventually be questioning the agents that were chasing a dark cab with four occupants. They'll want to know the start point of the chase, where the race went, and the end point." Slade said with darkness in his black eyes.

Gary shook his head and said, "So you think it will be that exhaustive?"

"It'll even be more intensive than that." Jake said, and went on before answering Gary's next question. The authorities will have teams of agents walking the chase route to collect anything that looks remotely plausible to the situation. It could be anything including gum wrappers, eaten food and especially spent shells. They be looking for any items that may contain DNA evidence."

"How long do you suppose the chase route was?" Gary asked Jake. "Oh about a mile. And they may even asked some of the neighbors if they saw anything out of the ordinary."

Gary thought for a minute to add up all the pieces and guesstimated how much time that would take and said, "the authorities will be busy for quite some time. Don't you think?"

'Don't be too sure about that," Slade questioned. "The Russians are really good at putting the pieces to together. You have to remember that their government is very suspicious during normal times, and now well you can do your own summation."

"Wow!" was the only thing that Gary could muster.

"There's a lot to go through and uncover so I think we are good for a few days. The major problem I have," Jake said, "is that the chase started not too far from the hotel, which means they will check all reservations at the Crown. And if they think they can get a hold of these guys by doing this, they'll check all the hotels and motels within a five mile radius."

They dropped the old Ford Soller about a two miles from the Crown Plaza, and before they left they thoroughly wiped it down and hoofed the rest of the way back to the hotel. They all arrived at different times and met up in Jake's room.

"I just spoke with James and he will send Dave Cuttings back here in one hour to move us to a safe house. He'll also bring us new Ids. In the meantime I want everyone to thoroughly clean your rooms, and I mean make them sterile. After that, we will check out and wait outside for Dave to show up."

Slade shook his head and asked Jake about the new plans. "No can do, partner. You'll have to wait until we are pulling away in Dave's car before you know more. I want to get this done quickly since we don't know how far the FSB is behind us. Let's get crackin'."

SIXTY-SIX

Getting Out

After Dave picked them up, the plans were changed again. Instead of going to another safe house, they were going to Finland via the Bay of Finland. The ferry system was only 160 miles from Saint Petersburg and if they did this directly and quickly they would be in Finland before anyone knew. Radke wanted them out of Russia as soon as possible and he was willing to gamble this time, in order to keep Russia off balance and his agents safe. Once they get to the Finland side they would take route 6 to Helsinki. It's about a 6 hour drive but with Dave behind the wheel of the big Ford, he should make it in little less than 5 hours. Once there, Lucas Cane, an attaché working for the American Embassy in Helsinki, will meet the three at Finavia International Airport and give them business class tickets to fly on a Boeing 787-8 Dreamliner back home to Reagan International Airport in Washington, D.C. The flight will take about 9 hours and once home, they will meet immediately with James and the rest of the staff at the Nebraska Complex at 11pm. They will have much to discuss and plan for the next phase of the operation. Once initiated all hell will break loose and the they hope and pray, that they will have enough time and confusion to stave of World War III.

SIXTY-SEVEN

FSB II

Lev Ivanov the special agent in charge of the northern district was telling the assistant director, Dr. Boris Andreev of the near capture of the wanted fugitives who were staying at the Crown Plaza hotel in Saint Petersburg. There was now a reward of $5,000 American dollars in Russian rubles for information leading to the arrest and conviction of the fugitives. Just like the FBI in America, the FSB operates the same way.

"Sir, we almost corralled them at the Crown Plaza. We missed them by six hours."

"How did you know it was them?" Dr. Boris Andreev said in a skeptical voice.

"Our agents who were chasing them personally identified them. We also have their visa's and photographs." Lev said, with concern in his voice. Lev was a long time FSB agent with a stellar record and in no way would he let these three get through his dragnet.

"Have you run their photos and visas through our national database, and if so have you found anything that would facilitate finding them?" Dr. Andreev asked, with a hollow voice.

"I'm afraid not, sir. It's almost like we're chasing ghosts, but to be honest their passports, visas and other information are no doubt fictitious." Lev said while getting up from his deck, in order to pace. He looked out his window from his office on the first floor of the Kremlin and of course it was still snowing and no doubt getting colder. It was the first week in December and the leaves left their presents of thoughts of summer long ago. He thought about having a drink, but it was too early even by Moscow standards. Now, if he was in Eastern Russia, let's say Siberia, he could drink all day long and nobody would think the worse of it.

"Did they leave any forwarding address or messages?" Boris asked.

"No of course not. We don't know who they really are or where they are from. However, all three spoke Russian."

"Well, there's your answer. They're Russian and no doubt live here. They were probably just snooping around to see if there was any significant information they could sell. After all, there was a Lada next to the Benz and I bet one of them own it. They are poor like most Russians and are trying to eke out a living anyway they can." Boris said with finality in his voice.

"No I don't think so, sir. First of all how did these poor souls get past the three check points to get to the Science and Technology buildings. Second, how did they have the knowledge to hot wire the Benz, sir. Third, we have traced their travels through their visa registrations and since they arrived in Moscow in November, they have went to Yerma, and then to Severodvinsk and now to Saint Petersburg.

"You have a point, Lev, and you say they went to Severodvinsk?" Dr. Andreev said with a heavy voice. He thought for a moment and realized that is where Russia designs and develops their latest nuclear submarines. "Okay, Lev, I think we have something here. This might turn into a national security issue. Wait a minute, if one was to visit one of the nuclear submarine sites; don't they need a special permit for this?"

"Yes they do." Lev said in an animated voice. "I'll check the permits for the last couple of weeks and see if any of the registration numbers on the permits match the numbers on the visas. Anything else, sir?"

"No that's it for now. Good hunting, Lev. Keep up the good work." The line went dead.

Boris sat back in his leather chair to get his considerable bulk comfortable. He wondered what motives the fugitives had. It could be as docile as snooping around as some tourists do. On the other hand it could be very sinister as discussed with Lev—a matter of national security. If these three have not been found in the next couple of days, or so, he would apply more heat and raise the amount to $10,000 American dollars. Of course every scatter head would be calling the tip lines to offer information.

SIXTY-EIGHT

Nebraska Complex Meeting

Once again, Jake, Slade and Gary, after arriving to the large conference corner room on the seventh floor of the Nebraska Complex, saw that the Secretary of the Department of Homeland Security, Mary Stinson, was attendance, even though it was 11pm Eastern time. Also, the Deputy Director, James Radke, was there. Everyone was on edge and you really couldn't blame them including the Secretary to be nervous. After everyone was there and seated, Mary stood at the head of the table, looked at everyone and began. "Again, I am attending your meeting, and again it is with grave concern. What we have at stake here is no less than our Democracy disappearing. We cannot and will not allow our country and Democracy go up in flames. If it happens we will let nearly 250 years of our forefathers, sweat, blood and lives go in vain. People, this cannot happen at any cost and as far as I'm concern it is set in stone.

Mary paused and leveled her look, with a stern awareness at everyone in the room and saw nothing less than ashen faces and trembling lips. She was a large woman, big raw boned, dark brown eyes and a flowing black mane of Jewish Descent. When she spoke you better listen, lest you get fire from her eyes and brutality from her voice. Yes that is the kind of woman she was, and that's why she was picked to head the Department of Homeland Security to put it simply. "Okay, I will now turn control of the meeting to James. You got the floor, sir."

As James rose from his seat, he briefly turned to the bank of windows and saw that the sleet was turning to snow from the street lights below. He needed the time to gather the rest of his thoughts. He knew this was for all the chips, so it better be perfect. He leaned his short wiry frame at everyone sitting at the table and began.

"Thank you madam Secretary," James said while looking at her from across the large table and getting the customary nod. "You have set the tone for this meeting and I am sure that everyone agrees." He saw that the attendees were nodding their heads. "Let's go, Jake. I want to hear everything."

"Well, sir after arriving at Moscow, we went to Moscow State University (MSU) and inserted the quantum flash drives in three different places to extract their present level of knowledge in quantum mechanics and computing science." Jake thought, *he wasn't going to clutter the information with the chase. He knew his boss well enough not to sweat the small stuff.* "Gary read the information from the drives and found that Russia was far behind us in this area. So our mission changed to concentrate on Russia while the Israeli Mossad handled Iran. Going on we went to Yerma to disable their old analog based ICBM"… Jake went on and told James and the group what happened while they were in Russia. He finished with… "sir after inserting the Stuxnet II virus flash drive into the USB port in the control panel on the bridge of the Maxim Gorky dry-docked for repairs at the Admiralty shipyards in Saint Petersburg, we checked out at the Crown Plaza. Dave then drove us to the west ferry terminus of the Bay of Finland. He stuck with us and then drove us to Helsinki. There Lucas Cane an attaché at the American Embassy met us at Finavia International Airport and gave us our business class ticket to Reagan International Airport."

"So I take it that everything went pretty smoothly except for the snafu in Severodvinsk?" The deputy secretary asked with his brown eyes blazing.

Jake momentarily stiffened and answered, "yes sir" as if he was saluting the retired colonel.

James looked squarely at Jake and said, "please go on."

"Sir, the only thing that worries me is the FSB. They know that there were three males in Russia that landed in Moscow and traveled to various places in the country. I'm not sure if they believed that we were tourist. Sure, going to Saint Petersburg was well with the tourists' purview, but Yerma and especially Severodvinsk I don't think so. Plus, they almost caught us outside the train depot in Saint Petersburg. Giving it more thought, though, they may think we are Russians because not once anyone heard us speak English. We acted like Russians, drank like Russians and spoke like Russians."

James now directed his attention to the Israeli nuclear scientist, Gary Zimmerman. "Gary, have you heard anything on the contrary from Yuri or Andrei?" James asked, while looking into the little guy's brown eyes.

"No sir—nothing. I think we pulled it off perfectly as he looked at Jake and Slade for their approval. Both black ops nodded their heads in agreement.

"Well I guess we will be ready to execute the final phase in three months or so. This will allow the Russian FSB to cool their jets and also give us time to develop and test our personnel transfer carriers on our mocked up Russian nuclear submarines. We need to be sure that these carriers work properly in transferring people from their subs to our vessels."

James looked at the Israeli nuclear scientist again and asked, " how long can our virus lay dormant."

"As long as we want. As long as they are napping there isn't any quantifiable loss of energy."

"Excellent!" the deputy secretary said with animation in his voice for the first time. James, looked at everyone in attendance as if to asked is there anything else and everyone remained silent. He next looked at the Secretary and asked if she had any more comments or questions, and she shook her head no. The Secretary then ended the meeting. As everyone was filing out, James motioned for Jake to hang back.

SIXTY-NINE

Heart-To-Heart

"Jake, do you want another cup of swill or anything?" The boss asked. "No sir, I'm fine. And more coffee at this hour would just keep me awake."

"How long have you been working for the Department of Homeland Security?"

"About eleven years. First with David Peterson and then with you, sir. I know what this is about. I screwed up and I have been beating up myself ever since the mistake."

"I'm sure you have. But orders and protocol have to be followed to the letter of the law, and you know that."

"I know that, sir. But the train arrived late in Severodvinsk and we were already on a tight schedule. So I improvised the situation to save time and decided to steal a flatbed truck instead of renting one. It was my call and I am solely responsible for it. Slade and Gary had nothing to do with it."

"I see that the Marine's 'Semper Fidelis' came out in you under these circumstances, and you took the best course of action. Hell, I probably would have done the same. But the thing that bothered me the most is you should have communicated with me when you knew the train would be arriving late. That would have given us time to accommodate the short time frame and figure out something."

"You're right, sir. I put the whole operation in jeopardy because of my stupidity. I won't let this happen again, sir. I believe it's the first mark on my record since working for DHS."

"There will be no formal reprimand or mark on your record. Heck, you're one of the best we have, but damn it, follow protocol and orders, Jake."

"I will, sir, and you can count on me. My word is my bond and you know it."

"Good. Now let's discuss plans for the Navy."

SEVENTY

FSB–Getting Closer

The assistant director of the FSB, had his secretary punch through to his special agent in charge for the Northern district. On the third ring, Lev picked up and said, "yes."

"This is Dr. Boris Andreev, Lev," Boris said in a matter-of-fact tone.

"Yes doctor, I was going to call you." Lev continued on. "We check the special permit registration numbers against the visas for the last week to be sure. We know the so-called three tourist arrived from Yerma to Severodvinsk on November 27th. We found there was three consecutive special permit numbers that matched three consecutive visa registration numbers, for the Okolnaya submarine base. I called the commandant at the base to see if the permits with those registration numbers showed up. He indicated no, and wanted to know what this was all about. I told him to watch the news. Now the question begs who authorized these permits and why."

"Lev, have you received any other information about this?"

"Well, yes I have. The three tourist that landed in Moscow in early November were males. In Yerma, they were identified as males. But when they went through the checkpoint coming into Severodvinsk and then going through the checkpoint leaving town, it wasn't three males. It was two tall males with a shorter female. At this point, I think they were on to us, with us knowing their general description. So one of them, the short one, dressed as a female to guarantee their passage through the checkpoint. And another thing, and this may be or may not be connected to our investigation, but an old KamAZ flatbed truck was stolen from the parking lot of where they were supposed to go and, so far, it hasn't resurfaced."

"Why would three tourists be interested in the design and development of our nuclear submarines? Very strange. I'm almost sure that these people aren't tourist.

Because of this these three must be turn coats wanting to sell the latest information to the West. Okay, I am now going to raise the amount of money to $10,000 American dollars and see if this helps to gain any useful information. And Lev, I want you to find the person that authorized the special permits for these people. Once we find this out, it will go a long ways in discovering what is going on."

"Sir, doubling the reward money may also give us that information."

"That's a good point, Lev, and I now know this is about national security," Dr. Andreev said with deep concern in his brown eyes, then he dropped the connection.

Dr. Andreev got up from his large oak desk and began to pace. Lordy, he needed the exorcise, even if it was just walking. He couldn't believe what was going on. Remembering, this has to be a very strange set of events. *We will catch the intruders*, he thought.

SEVENTY-ONE

Cabinet Level Meeting (Sea Going)

The DHS Secretary, Mary Stinson, was at a Cabinet meeting in DC with the Chairman of the Joint Chiefs of Staff, Alfonso Grove, and other senior military officers to discuss the latest strategy of mission Darkfall. The Navy had a full complement of high ranking officers here since they were the lead in this operation. Alfonso was at the head of the large table directing the discussions. He looked at everyone and gaveled the meeting to order.

"Okay we all know this is paramount to the planet earth surviving and mistakes cannot be made. Let's hear the latest developments and strategies on this mission.

Rear Admiral Elisabeth Anne Fessler stood up and squared her shoulders before speaking. She was a short woman with deep brown eyes, flaxen hair and a powerful voice. "Sir, I've been working closely with Commander, Dennis Carlson, in regards to developing personnel transfer carriers to retrofit most of the Russian Navy subs that will be submerged when we actively stagger the Stuxnet II virus, both on land and sea. For the seagoing effort the virus will reduce their nuclear reactors to half power and this will also cause the same effect for their propulsion systems. More importantly all of their nuclear missiles and warheads will be totally disarmed. Quite a feat I must say."

"Enough of the theatrics, Elizabeth." the chairman indicated with a scowl on his face. He was a big, dark haired American Italian that rose through the ranks the hard way. *No siree,* he thought. *His skids were not greased and no fancy schools just like his friend, Frank Mulligan, and after all these years they still stayed in touch.*

"Sorry, sir. Now I'll turn over the meeting to Commander Carlson who has been heavily involved in the design, development and production of these collars.

"Sir, everything is going smoothly except for the latest design of collars for their newest nuclear submarines. Most of their collars are universal, especially for the older nuclear submarines. But they changed designs for the new classes like the Arcturus class, the Yasen I, II, III class and the Borei class. Essentially these are Russia's new generation of nuclear submarines since the cold war."

"Are you saying that you haven't developed any collars for any of the new subs?" The chairman said, with alarm in his voice.

"No, sir, that's not what I said. We have all the designs, which are mostly universal, except for the latest Arcturus class. Also, there is no way to 100% test these collars since we have no real Russian nuclear subs to test. We only have mock ups and their okay. As you know, when the virus works on their propulsion systems it will only allow them half power. If we can't transfer them submerged, they can always ascend to the surface. Like all their technology, including ours, it's highly secretive and always has been. Therein lies the difficulty."

"Yes it has commander and probably always will." The chairman said with wishful intentions. Now let's double our efforts and find the new collar design for their latest Arcturus class nuclear submarines.

"We will sir!" commander Carlson emphasized.

"Now what about communications? Has all of their c-lines and focal points been discovered. I mean their c-lines and all their originations and departing locations." The chairman looked around the large room and saw the Navy Captain rise from his seat.

"Sir, we have located the two primary communication centers that the Russian Navy use. One is in the suburbs of Moscow and the other one is the Maxim Gorky ship currently dry-docked at the Admiralty shipyards in Saint Petersburg. Mary, you want to help us out here?" The Captain asked, since he knew DHS was the clearing house and was very intimate on this part of the operation.

The Secretary of the Department of Homeland Security (DHS), Mary Stinson, rose and thanked the captain for his participation. "I know most of you here know quite a few details of the mission, so I will briefly point out the important points. The Russian Navy mainly communicates via sonar, just like we do, for their submerged subs. They also have many c-lines embedded on the sea floor to handle some of their communications. Of course these are within their domain. Their subs merely need to get close to these lines to collect information. Once they surface they have a myriad ways to communicate. Now the important part. They have two primary points to send and receive information. The first one is in the Crimea for the Black Sea. Arrangements have already been made for this communication center. The second one is on a destroyer commissioned the Maxim Gorky and is currently dry-docked for maintenance and repairs at the Admiralty shipyard in Saint Petersburg as previous mentioned by the captain. Three of our operatives attacked the ship and basically made it look like it was squadron. The distractions were well placed and seemed as real as they get. This bought time for our people to get to the bridge and insert the virus into one of their control panels. It went beautifully. Now, the Stuxnet II virus is lying dormant waiting to be activated." Mary looked around the table and it appeared that everyone understood. "Are there questions or comments from anyone?"

"Did everyone get out and away unseen?" Rear Admiral, Elizabeth Anne Fessler, asked with intense brown eyes.

"Yes the operation was well planned and everyone got out clean. Now, are there any other questions?" Mary asked with her dark eyes intently looking at everyone.

The Rear Admiral continued to stand. "Mary, what about the Crimea operation? Is there any crucial information we need?"

"No, as I said the arrangements have already been made for Crimea."

"But because of the paramount nature of Darkfall we need to know the details." Elisabeth said, frowning.

Mary, thought for a long moment and finally said, "if everyone must know, the Mossad is involved with this operation. And I'm ending this with enough said."

The room was quiet, so Mary deferred and turned the meeting over to Alfonso Grove, The Joint Chiefs of Staff.

General Grove rose from his chair at the head of the table and asked if there were any additional questions; there weren't. He gaveled the heavy table and adjured the meeting.

SEVENTY-TWO

Afterward

After the meeting was adjourned and most everyone left, Mary Stinson, Alfonso Grove and David Coswell stayed behind and waited for the Secretary of Defense to show up. This time of the day D.C. was awash in traffic. The four need to personally get together to discuss this further. The Army, Marines and Air Force would meet later in another Cabinet meeting. Afterword, President Trump would be notified of the results. He was particularly interested, because of the importance of the mission. If successful, he would go down as one of the most influential President's in history, However, no one would know about this in order to keep peace in the world.

When Jerome Orson walk in to the room, everyone stood and went to meet him, and Mary gave him a big hug. He was in the loop and very important to the success of Darkfall. After all the pleasantries concluded, everyone took their seats and Mary Stinson was the first to speak. "Jerome, are the armed forces ready to engage if needed?" Mary asked with her dark brown eyes drilling into him.

"Mary we're progressing. As you know this is a huge and monumental job getting all of our armed forces on standby if this goes South. We all know where we'll be heading. So to give us the edge of surprise, in either case, we need to do this with as much stealth as possible and go about it nonchalantly. Preparing for an all-out nuclear war with Russia will bring in all the big three of the evil axis. And as we all know this is a lose-lose situation. Studies have shown the initial shock wave and subsequent nuclear winters will reduce the planet's population by ninety percent at least. And everyday, the remaining few will have to give it a massive effort just to get to the next day. It's just horrible.

"We know," Alfonso Grove the Joint Chiefs of Staff, said with grave concern in his deep brown eyes, "We all will be safe 2000 feet under the surface of the Colorado mountains near Colorado Springs in the Cheyenne Complex. We recently expanded the facility to hold 20,000 individuals. And as before, it will depend on a few important factors if they are registered and allowed in. We initially will have food for the first three years and after that, we can grow our own food under artificial light that mimics the sun. Of course, it will be a city with its own infrastructure. No one without protective gear will be able to go outside for many generations. By then, what we look like and act like is anybody's guess."

"But we don't want that!" Jerome said, "What kind of person is looking at pictures of what the earth used to be? Sure, we can watch movies and stream until we are sick in the face. Popcorn and Coke are entertainment. We can exercise and use most of the facilities of our little city. We'll have cameras and sounds of what it looks like, but we can't go outside. What a way to live!" Jerome looked directly at Mary and asked her if this will work because, this time, they were betting all the marbles.

Mary thought for a long moment to gather her thoughts before excoriating some of the men in the room. "Come on, you're all gloom and doom because you don't think this will work. Of course, it will!...or President Trump would never give his approval on such a thing. He told me himself how he wants this mission to progress. He wants to make sure so he broke the cabinet meeting into three. One basically for the Navy for sea going operations, in which we just had, and one for the land-based missiles that involved the Army and the Marines, along with the Air Force and Space Force and Coast Guard. The third will be chaired by President Trump. Going on, we have already checked the Russian satellites and not one has high enough radiation levels to indicate they could fire nuclear missiles from any of their satellites."

Jerome broke in. "Yes, we checked all of the Russian satellites that could possibly fire missiles under the pretense of maintaining the International Space Station (ISS) and Elon Musk has test fired some of his rockets to double checked the Russian satellites and they're all clean. Of course, they are bristling with very high resolution cameras to confirm this question. Also, his Starlink system flying thousands of satellites in low earth orbit has been checking Russia's lower orbiting satellites for months. The higher orbiting satellites Russia has, like I said, has been checked with Elon's missile test firings."

Alfonso Grove looked around the table and saw that everyone was quiet, so he gaveled the meeting to adjournment. The chairman looked around again and said, "Do I hear a second?"

"I second the motion," David Coswell, the Admiral of the Navy, said. As they all walked out David got alongside Mary to ask her a few additional questions. "Mary, your agency is the clearing house for this since your team is directly responsible for the success of Darkfall. Are you sure that everything is in order?"

"David, I have my best team working on this, and my Deputy Secretary, James Radke, has assured me more than once that everything is up to snuff. You know your guys still have some work to do on the personnel transfer carriers (PTC)," Mary indicated.

"I know this and it will be taken care of long before the virus is activated. And be assured that we will have all six flat tops roaming the seas with some Russian speaking captains aboard."

"Just wanted confirmation, David," Mary said, with her near black eyes boring into David's face.

"You got it, Madam Secretary."

SEVENTY-THREE

Surprise!

"Zoey, what a surprise. Now wait a minute. I apologize for not calling you sooner, but as you know I've been busy with another mission in Russia. I just got home a few days ago and haven't even unpacked because of all the meetings I have attended. No don't ask. This is double top secret. No, there is nothing for you to do on this one. Oh, one thing though, you can get your sexy bod over here. Yes, thank God, I have a few days off before I'm back on the chain gang. I'm calling up the incoming flights now from Logan to Reagan."

"No, no sweetheart. I don't want to go through Reagan because of the air disaster awhile back. Look up Dulles for my flight. I know it's a little longer drive for you, but I know you want me safe and secure for you," she said as she giggled.

"I'm thinking I want you warm too!" Jake emphasized with a sly look on his face.

"Well that's a given, honey. What do the flights look like?"

"Can you take a couple days off for the romper room?" Jake said, with wicked thoughts running around in his head. Oh, darn It's past October so I can't have a Goth head running around. Remember last year–it was so cool," Jake said with a devilish look on his face."

"Are you sneering at me?"

"No that's my naughty grin." Okay, how about Dulles at 10 am on Saturday. Will that work for you? That way will have Saturday through next Tuesday."

"OOOOH! that sounds delicious babe. You have any special plans for us?" Zoey inquired.

"I'll think of something, sweets, you know that."

"Well you don't have much time, so get crackin'." Zoey said in a forceful, yet playful manner. "I'll tell you what, you're a gamblin' man, right? So I'll bet my surprise against yours, and will see who wins. When I get there, it'll be your call." Zoey said, with her beautiful blue eyes a sparkling.

"You're on, Zip." They said their goodbyes and hung up. Jake sat back on his couch and wondered what her surprise was. His brain was already overloaded with what's going on and now this. But this he likes!

SEVENTY-FOUR

More FSB Information

The assistant director, Dr. Boris Andreev, placed an urgent call to his special agent in charge, for the Northern district, Lev Ivanov. "Good morning, Lev. How goes the battle."

"Fine, sir. I was just going to call. We have uncovered more information."

"It's about times, so what do you have and I hope it's good, because the director is breathing down my neck. As you know we have increased the reward to $10,000 American dollars. That's a lot of money for us poor Russians, although the money will not be released until there is a conviction."

"So what's going on, Lev?" Dr. Andreev asked while having another sip of Stoli. It was 9am, but he didn't care. The pressure on him from the director was enormous. He knew by 5pm he would be polluted, but would still have another two hours to slide by. After that he wouldn't be good for any completed sentences. It was a good thing his condo was close by. Once home, his wife would greet him with whatever–*what a life* he thought.

"Dr. Andreev we finally got good information from one of our tip lines. Doubling the reward amount must have helped," Lev said, with animation in his voice. Normally, he spoke like a robot.

"Well get on with it!" Dr. Andreev huffed.

Lev Ivanov thought for a minute before he went on. "We have the name of Pavel Volkov, a welder that works for one of the nuclear submarine yards in Severodvinsk."

"That makes sense, Lev. Did you concentrate on the other two yards before this?"

"No."

"Why didn't you check the other yards. After all the three yards could be related!" Dr. Andreev huffed.

"No, all the information was coming from Sevmash, so we were directing our resources there. A friend of his that works at the same yard heard and saw the appeal on national television. He remembered that Pavel told him it wouldn't be long before he would be $10,000 American richer. He put two and two together and figured that it was Pavel. He must have taken three blank permits and gave them to a contact to fill them out officially."

"These permits are laying around on benches in the sub shops?" Dr. Andreev said in amazement. "I thought they were locked up and had to go through official channels to be okayed and issued."

"I thought so too, sir"

"This has to stop now! I'll get to the proper authorities and have this taken care of." Boris took another sip of his vodka and thought about what he would say next. Is Pavel around?" Boris asked.

"No, we have been checking everywhere. He hasn't been at work for the last two days, and his wife and kids haven't seen him either."

"Okay we need to run a background check on Pavel and see what we come up with. I want it yesterday. You hear me Lev!"

"Yes sir."

"What about his contact? What's his name?"

"Sir, his name is Marlen Alex, and you're not going to like this, but we can't find him either." Lev said, with a slight quiver in his voice.

"Good Lord, what is going on here. What did Mr. Alex do?" Dr. Andreev *wondered as the well of information was getting deeper.*

"He was a line supervisor at the same sub shop that Pavel worked at."

"Which shop was that?"

"Just a minute sir, I have to grab my notes." After a minute he came back.

"I think it's Sevmash. Although there are other shipyards there that are less important."

"How come you are referring to Pavel in past tense, well wouldn't you!" Dr. Andreev roared. "You also need to do a background check on this Alex character. I want to know everything."

Lev thought about the many scenarios and finally came back, "I guess so."

Another sip and another command. "There's no guess so about it! We need to scour every submarine shipyard to see if there is more useful information. Lev, we got to get down to the bottom of this. I have a haunch this is way more important than we think. I think I will advise the Director to increase security detail for all of us, including all the special agents in charge. It appears murder is not past their purview. I wonder how high this goes up; hence the additional security. I feel that we are running out of time for something, and I wish I knew what it was."

SEVENTY-FIVE

It's A Surprise

Jake got up extra early on Saturday, the day he was going to meet his sweetheart, Zoey Chamberlain. He was so excited, he couldn't sleep. Before he shaved and took his shower, he went out to his garage with his bathrobe on, to decide which car he wanted to collect her in. He usually picked her up in the company Ford, but this time he really wanted to surprise her. It had been nearly three months since he last saw her. He kept in touch with her on his private smart phone from time-to-time, but that wasn't nearly enough. He wanted to see her flowing sable brown hair, beautiful face with her sharp blue eyes and luscious red lips. He wanted to hold her and run his hands over her gorgeous figure. They were perfect for each other. It was 11:00 am when they pulled into Jake's driveway. Jake let her out, grabbed her luggage and led her in to the house.

"Sure smells wonderful in here. Are you making something, honey," Zoey commented.

"Ya, I had a hard time between a good baked casserole Frittata or a zucchini/ sausage roll."

"It sure smells good."

"Can you tell which one, Zip?" Jake kidded with his famous smile.

"Oh come on, sweet buns, my olfactory nodes are not that sophisticated," Zoey spun and gave Jake her gorgeous blue eyes.

"Well, baked casserole Frittata won out." He took it out of the Fridge and slipped it into the oven." It'll take about 40 minutes, and in the meantime I'm going to prepare and bake some biscuits with honey that'll you'll love. Come on and help me sweetie."

As they were working together in the kitchen, they caught up with what they were doing. Zoey was telling Jake that she was now a director at Fidelity in Boston. She told him that she was responsible for a whole department that included fifty analysts. A big job with lots of responsibility.

"How do you like it?" Jake asked.

"It's good, but some days it can be hectic."

"I know the feeling. I can't tell you much about what I'm doing, only to say it's big, really big! And in one of the phases I screwed up that could've brought down the whole agency."

"No!" Zoey, exclaimed. "Are you alright?"

"Ya, we got lucky," Jake said as he squeezed her waist.

"You keep doing that, hon, and the wild cat will come out in me?"

After breakfast they relaxed on one of the couches and continued their conversation. Zoey got near Jake's right ear and whispered. "I got a surprise for you."

He thought for a moment. "Ah you got me a present, you little devil. What is it?'

"It's a present alright, but it's the kind we'll love and it will stay with us for the rest of our lives."

"What's that mean?"

Zoey leaned in again–"we're having a baby, honey." Jake's blue eyes snapped as he got off the couch to let the news sink in.

"We are!" he exclaimed.

"You're going to be a daddy."

He pulled her off the couch, embraced her and gave her a long deep kiss on her luscious red lips. "When?" he asked.

"About seven months," Zoey said with an animated voice.

"Do we know the sex yet?"

"No, sweets. I thought we would find out together or just wait for the happy event to happen."

Jake spun her around and looked into her beautiful blue eyes and said, "I'll be darned. I'm going to be a daddy!"

"Yes, you are," Zip said, as a broad smile broke out on both of their faces. They headed upstairs to consummate the news.

SEVENTY-SIX

Cabinet Level Meeting (Land)

The meeting began with the rap of the gavel. All military dignitaries were there that were involved with land warfare. Also, Mary Stenson, Secretary of the Department of Homeland Security (DHS) was in attendance with Jerome Orson, Secretary of the Department of Defense (DOD). Further, there were other high ranking military officers present that were critical for the dissemination of the latest information. The meeting was just as important as the sea going meeting held a week ago. Again, Alfonso Grove the Chair of the Joint Chiefs of Staff opened the meeting.

"Okay, you all have your swill?" Alfonso asked. Everyone nodded their heads. "I think I'll have Mary lead off since her department is the clearing house and has all information available for mission Darkfall. Okay, Mary, you have the floor."

"First, I know most of you here and you know how vitally important this is. The sea going portion was held last week and now it's our turn. It doesn't matter about one-upmanship or anything else. All of your phones and recording devices are locked in a room in a different building just like last week, and you understand why we had to take these steps." Everyone nodded.

"This is so damn important and if we fail we'll all be heading to the Cheyenne facility and generations of us will spend the rest of our lives there. So listen up." Mary leveled her deep brown eyes at everyone before she continued. "Like the sea going operation, Russia has two main land based communication centers for their missiles. One is located in the suburb of Moscow and is called Kuntsevo. The other is under the Urals in the Kosvinsky mountain range. They also have two older missile silos based on older Analog technology. We have already taken these out. The other installations are digital and will be disarmed by the new Stuxnet II virus. And I don't need to remind you that this is top secret information and will remain in this room. Are we all in agreement?" Everyone nodded again. "We are not here for the particulars just the big story." She looked at everyone again and paused before she resumed. "The virus's smart drives have been inserted for both land and sea going operations. Right now they lay dormant waiting to be executed. And this will be done on a slightly staggered basis. In the end Russia won't know what hit them. But they will be madder than hornets. Their military and civilian systems will go on high alert and because of the nature of the attacks, thousands if not millions of their best software engineers and programmers will be all over the code that controls these systems like white on rice. All of their media and television programming will be controlled by the FSB and their civil liberties will become nonexistent. It will be locked down and basically become a dystopian society with no one above suspicion until this event or calamity is identified. The worry about this is the Russian society will never get back to where they use to be. I know if I was in their boots I probably would be using the same method. And knowing Russia this is only the beginning. Any questions?" Mary asked.

The four star general, the commandant of the Marines, Juan Rivera, stood and said, "you know the Russians will come for us right away. They'll think that we are the only ones that have this kind of technology."

"No not necessarily," Mary chimed in. "That's why we have staggered the attack to measure their reaction before going further." Mary stepped back a step or two from the bristling Juan Rivera "Now by staggering the attack it will give us some time to measure their reactions very intimately. And they will not come for us, because there is a definite reason why!" Mary said emphatically.

Everyone looked at Juan and Mary with rapt attention. The room was so quiet you could hear a pin drop. "Why is this so!" Juan challenged. He went on, "it seems that this is straight out of Star Wars."

"Your statement is not far off. However, I'm not at liberty to tell you or anyone else if you're wondering. You'll find out at the next meeting when the President will be there." With that you could hear a low whistle emanating around the room.

Jerome Orson of the Department of Defense (DOD) stood up and looked at everyone in the room. "You all heard what Mary Stinson said and there better not be any leaks, because I promise you we will hunt you down and take you to Gitmo–it's open again! And you don't want to go there and you all know why. Even though most in the room were high ranking, they all looked at Jerome with ashen faces and nodded. "Now, if there are no other questions…"

"There's one question, sir," Colonel Saunders asked.

"Yes, Robert. What's burning your craw?" Jerome asserted.

"How come there are two meetings instead of one?" the colonel inquired.

"Well, as Mary Stinson indicated, this operation is so critical we need two cabinet meetings. This idea went all the way to President Trump. He then indicated he wanted this split into two cabinet level meetings. He thought by doing this, the information would be disseminated better and therefore be carried by each person more clearly. And to tell you the truth, I believe the President was right. The Secretary of Defense looked around the room again and issued the same question. Is there anything else?" The room remained silent. "Okay, I'll give control back to Alfonso and he will gavel the meeting closed."

SEVENTY-SEVEN

Any New Findings?

The assistant director, Dr. Boris Andreev sat in his cushy leather chair and looked through his large window at the falling snow. Christmas was around the corner and he had a lot of things to do according to his wife, Eva. He knew he had to cut down on his drinking, or he would never get the list done. Christmas or no Christmas he had to solve the current problem. The media had turned the issue into an national event. Once they discovered it could be a national security situation, the media was like a bull dog and wouldn't let go. Now Putin was involved and that turned up the pressure enormously.

Boris called and said, "good morning Lev, and how are you doing today?" Dr. Andreev inquired.

"Doing fine, and thank you for the fine Colombian coffee you sent me. In fact I'm enjoying a cup of it now. Good stuff, sir."

"I'm glad you like it. Now have you found out anything more about the sub issue?" He was hoping for something, anything useful.

"We have thoroughly checked Pavel's friends, his banking, his wife's bank accounts, where they live at and his work associates. He's clean and lives like many of us, drives an old car, loves his wife and attends church services sometimes. No, there are no dark secrets behind him. We have found a note that was passed from Pavel to Marlen."

"Well, I'm waiting–get on with it."

Pavel recited the short note to his boss.

"We have forensics looking at it now. Possibly, if we can lift a fingerprint off the paper and if it isn't Pavel's or Marlen's we'll have a lead to another person." Lev acknowledged.

"Now what about Marlen Alex? Is there anything that would raise a suspicion of doubt that he was doing Russia harm?" The assistant director, quizzed.

"No, there isn't except to say that they have both vanished." Lev said with a sad voice as if lamenting about something.

"Is there any other information on this. I mean I'm exasperated about this issue. You do know that Putin has been alerted about this problem since it could lead to a national security issue. The director has given me to the first week in January, and if we can't solved this by then, Lev, you'll be working for a new assistant director."

"Really, Boris. I didn't know that. What's with the director?" Lev inquired.

"It's called Vladimir Putin. The director may lose his job too. It's just horrible. There's no way that Putin will let us out of his snare. If this happens, I hope it only involves losing our jobs. I'm so afraid of him that whatever you call him, he's still a dictator. I can think of various ways of being punished."

"What are you talking about?" Lev popped. Now he was worried too, because he was part of this investigation.

"Vladimir can do anything he wants. You have to remember he used to be a colonel in the KGB. He's a vicious dog and doesn't care about anything except Russia and maybe his family. I just hope he doesn't make me or the director an example of the FSB. I've seen a lot of people getting tried on trump up charges in a so-called court and some were sent to the Gulags in Siberia."

"He wouldn't do that!" Lev blurted.

"Oh yes he would, and if it strikes his fancy, like the monster he is, he will."

"Oh my God!" Lev declared. "I'll pray for you, Boris. But will figure this out."

"I hope so."

SEVENTY-EIGHT

Nebraska Complex
Seagoing

Again, the Secretary of Homeland Security, Mary Stinson, was at the meeting. She waited before everyone was seated with their sodas and coffee before she began. Lordy, what they were about to hear, they needed something stronger, much stronger. The Deputy Secretary, James Radke was there at the other end of the table along with Jake Cannon, Slade Swanson and Gary Zimmerman. Others in attendance were their database director and profiler, Tom Morrison, Dr. Tonia Franks, the computer guru, Dr. Clyde Ferris Homeland's neural net expert and Steve Olson, Homeland's logistics expert.

Mary leveled her deep brown eyes with a stern look across the table at everyone, and began with her low strong baritone voice. She boomed, "listen up". Everyone's head snapped to attention, and it was quiet now—so quiet you could hear a pin drop. "In the last two weeks I have attended two high level cabinet meetings. And I mean high level!" She empathized this with her brown eyes blazing. Before going on she thought deeply about what she was going to say next. "The first meeting was on the Russian Navy sea going technology. In other words, their capabilities and main communication points. The Joint Chiefs of Staff, Alfonso Grove, chaired the meeting. Even the Secretary of Defense (DOD) Jerome Orson was there. A strange sound summoned around the table after everyone heard this. Now since the Deputy Secretary of the Department of Homeland Security (DHS) has been thoroughly briefed, he will forward the meeting. Mary looked over at James with his hands behind his back, and with her eyes, she motioned for him to begin.

James unfolded is hands and laid them on the heavy oak table and leaned his short wiry frame toward the surface to gain everyone's attention and emphasis before he began. He was a smaller person, physically, than Mary but had all the savvy and power like she did.

"Okay, you all heard Mary, and I'm also here to tell you this will be the most important, top-secret meeting you will ever attend." Everyone was now looking at each other wondering what was coming next. "We started mission Darkfall, first, working with our nuclear scientist on loan from Israel, Gary Zimmerman and Israeli Mossad to take out Iran's nuclear facilities since they dropped out of the accord on October of 2023. However, since President Trump is again in office he will replace all sanctions on Iran. The previous administration seemed not to care. This gave Iran time and far more latitude to sell more oil, a lot more oil to their friends. This enabled Iran to finance their proxies with missiles to attack Israel. And Russia was giving them new technology on how to manufacture a nuclear warhead and explicitly load it with the right kind of explosives to set off a fission chain reaction that would culminate in an atomic explosion. The Russians were also teaching them how to design and develop the mechanics of inserting the nuclear warhead atop of one of their longest range missiles that could reach Western Europe and NATO. In addition to this nightmare, North Korea were sending some of their best army troops, weapons and equipment to Russia to help fight Ukraine."

The deputy secretary stopped and look around the room to gain their attention to their highest level, before refolding his hands behind his back. He walked over to the large east facing windows to see it continuing to snow and to gather his thoughts for the next salvo. For a split second he saw his to do Christmas list for his nieces and nephews. Even though he was a bachelor, he was part of a large family with seven siblings. He unfolded his hands, walked back to the table, and began again. "Okay, during the last administration's term, Iran had so much money selling their oil that they financed terrorists killings of many innocent people. They burned babies for everyone to see and rape women at will without any remorse. On October 7th, 2023 Humus and Hezbollah slaughtered 1200 Jewish people. It was the single most deadly killings since the Holocaust. And, President Trump still hasn't received all the hostages from this gruesome event. These people are not human, they are monsters. I hope the President will have the final say. I'm wondering how much technology Russia has given Iran. They are already using shot spotter in some of their major cities. And I know that they have advanced their drone technology. What's next? Because of all the help that was given to Iran from Russia we decided to change the course of direction of Darkfall. It has been now directed to Russia. We will let Mossad take care of Iran's nuclear facilities with the new Stuxnet II virus. In the meantime, we'll neutralize Russia's ability to strike with their nuclear warheads, submerged, on land and in the air."

"Sir, I don't want to interrupt but what about Russia's satellites?" Dr. Clyde Ferris ask.

"Oh you mean if some of them are armed with nuclear missiles." Good question, Clyde.

"With a major boost from Elon Musk's Starlink system and some help from NASA we already determined that they are all clean. However, if we would have waited another year or two, that probably wouldn't be the case. Now if there isn't…yes Jake." "What about China's satellites, sir?"

"There aren't too many of them yet. And, I not only mean satellites, but armed satellites as well. If they ever try such a foolish act they will certainly know they will get a major retaliation from us. Okay, we still have a lot to review so no more questions for now."

He continued. "So we sent our guys to Russia and that would be Jake, Gary and Slade with 30 day tourist visas that started close to mid-November. They got to their safe house and went to Moscow State University (MSU) to test the flash drives and they worked perfectly. From there, they went to Yerma to take down one of the two analog missile sites… " James finished up with speaking about infesting the Maxim Gorky with a Stuxnet II virus at the admiralty shipyards in Saint Petersburg.

Dr. Tonia Franks was the next to stand and inquire about this amazing story. "How did you make it out after doing all that damage?"

Slade stood and took the question. "We went northeast my dear in a very fast bullet proof embassy car and shoved off at the west terminus of the Bay of Finland. Once across we were escorted in the same hotrod to Helsinki in under five hours."

"Wow." was the only thing Tonia could say.

Slade continued, "We met at the airport with an embassy official and he handed our business class ticket to D.C. Nine and a half hours later, we were home via Finnair. Hell, a movie should be made about this!"

Mary stood up again and said, "Enough of this chatter. We still have a long way to go. We can have a 15-minute recess." Everyone nodded. "But no one will leave the seventh floor. There are restrooms here."

SEVENTY-NINE

Nebraska Complex
(Recess)

J ake walked outside the room to the nearest alcove, took a seat and used his personal smart phone to call Zoey. He was the only one to have a smart phone in their presence besides the Secretary and Deputy Secretary. He had been so excited since he had heard the news from her, that he was already buying things for the baby. He purchased a crib and a matching bassinet and a walkie talkie system for the house. That way they could always hear the little one from the alcove room he was building off the master bedroom. He even brought home a race car for a two year old to sit in and push. When Zoey heard about that she told him to take it back–that's too far in the future. He didn't take it back, he lined up the little Silver Ferrari with the rest of his muscle cars in his garage.

"Hey babe, what's crackin in bean town?" Jake inquired.

"Oh I didn't tell you yet. I accepted a lateral position with Fidelity in Alexandria."

"That's great, hon. When will you be starting?"

"In two weeks. Can you believe that!" Zip exclaimed. "You better hustle and get the house ready for the three of us."

"Wow that was fast!" Jake exclaimed.

"Well this wild cat moves fast when she wants to. I think we'll have a small garden wedding on your back lawn facing the Potomac. For the reception you have a large garage space we can use. Jake, you can't think bachelor anymore–you're going to be a married man and a father."

He was thinking about how fast some of his operations went, but nothing like this. Zoey almost had him speechless. "When are you getting back here?"

"Right after I wrap up my work here in about two weeks. I'm already decluttering and selling a few sticks of furniture from the small condo. I'll use the last weekend to clean and finish up the rental condo. I already reserved a U-Haul trailer for my RAV4. If I take it easy, I'll drive it in two days,"

"You want me to fly up and drive down with you?"

"Naw, I'm a big girl and can make it by myself. I just want you to have the house ready when I arrive. Oh, have you told any of your friends yet?"

"I will soon, hon. But, I have been extremely busy since I got back and haven't found the time yet."

"Well buster you better get moving."

"Okay sweets I will. They said their goodbyes. Now Jake was thinking about how he was going to manage this. *There was a lot of work to do. And what about his five muscle cars? He would have to store them for a while.* He thought. Well, he would have to put his organizer hat on and call in a few favors.

EIGHTY

Nebraska Complex Land Based

After the group were reseated in their chairs, Mary gaveled the meeting open again. "Remember this meeting is for the big picture to let all of you know what is going on and why. The globe has simply gotten too small and dangerous, and for the love of God our country is not going to sit back and let it be destroyed and all humanity perish. Our country has shed too much blood getting to where we are today. Hell, all the advance industrial nations feel the same way. Again, I must remind you that this meeting is top-secret and nothing gets beyond these walls. You will get your phones back after this discussion. Only three people were permitted their phones during recess and now they are locked up again. If you need any additional information after the meeting or in the coming days, please refer your question to James, Jake, Gary and Slade. They are the ones that know the full scope of the operation."

Mary took her right hand to pushed back her thick dark mane before turning the meeting over to the Deputy Secretary of the Department of Homeland Security (DHS), James Radke.

James, once again looked around the room and could see that everyone was riveted to what he was about to say. "Ladies and gentlemen, it's about time we take out one of the major players in the evil axis. By doing this, it will greatly weaken the remaining three, and the beauty is Russia will never know who did this to them. In essence, we take out the teeth of Russia's mother bear. Oh sure, they will have their conventional weapons left and some are quite major, but no nuclear capability on land, sea, or air." James could see that Tonia Franks wanted to speak and he headed her off. "Wait until this discussion is done before we take any questions" Everyone nodded. "Okay, where was I, oh yes. There was another land based analog silo missile located, in all places, Severodvinsk. That's where they design, develop and build their latest nuclear submarines. This was particularly hard to get to and disarm. We made it look like a bunch of meth heads broke in and carted off all the brass and metal to sell on their black market. Just like Yerma. Oh yes, Russia has the same problem as we do. So now with both of their old analog nukes gone we only needed to concentrate on their digital nuclear facilities. In itself, this was a tall order, but with the internet of the world it gave us a fighting chance. Of course the net is always growing, including the dark net." The Deputy Secretary stopped for a minute to drink some water, and to gather his next salvo. He remembered to keep it high level and to not get lost in the weeds. That's left to the big kilowatt guys like Dr. Clyde Ferris.

"We had some friends in Moscow who were treated very badly by Vladimir Putin. In one case, a family was hounded for years because of political dissonance. Eventually, the uncle was tried, tortured, and sent off to the gulags in Siberia. And, it wasn't long before his niece was poisoned. As it so happened, a very good friend of the family was an officer for the Rocket Strategic Forces (RSF) in Moscow. And through a third person, he was instructed on how to insert the USB flash drive and where to insert it in. Meaning, the control desk at the RSF Headquarters in Moscow. There was another place, but it was buried in the Urals. We have monitored Russia's Federal Security Service (FSB) and it still appears they are chasing their own tails. So in essence, the three Stuxnet II viruses are dormant and waiting are commands to set the quantum wolves out to feast."

"What about the other two locations?" Tonia Franks asked.

" You can talk to Jake about this later. But remember this is top secret and no one outside of this room will know about this. Understood."

"Yes, sir. Now what about Iran?" She asked again.

"I mean, what are you saying?" James inquired. "There are a couple of ways to look at this. With Russia out of the picture, Iran will be nothing more than a paper tiger."

"When and who is going to take out Iran, sir?"

"That's not your concern," James huffed. "Leave it alone!" Now if there are no more questions, I will turn it over to Mary. It's been a long day! Mary, it's all yours."

"Thanks, Mr. Deputy Secretary. While both James and I were speaking, I was running a thought over in my mind about a decision

I needed to make. So here it is, to make paramount, and even more paramount there will be one more meeting. And from our group, only myself, James, Jake, Gary and Slade will be in attendance in the situation room at the White House. I can't impress upon you enough, because if we fail we'll be all heading to the Cheyenne Mountain complex." With a gavel strike the meeting was adjourned. While everyone was leaving with ashen faces, Jake pulled Gary and Slade aside to meet him in his office.

EIGHTY-ONE

The Boys

As soon as they got into Jake's office, he spun around and with joy in his deep voice, said, "I've been wanting to tell you two for days, but we have been so busy that I hadn't found the right time. Slade please wait. So I'll just blurt it out. Zoey and I are getting married." Jake grinned.

Slade was to first to react. He walked up to his buddy, saluted, hugged him firmly, stepped back and gave him a hardy handshake. "We'll I was wondering when Zoey was going to get to you. You know you make a beautiful couple and no doubt will have beautiful kids."

Gary stood back for a while and just took in the scene. He could tell that they were really close friends.

"Talking about kids, I just found out Zip has one in the oven. Jake said, with great pride in his voice."

Gary walked up and shook his hand. "Congratulations buddy! It's a privilege to know you, and I want you to know that it is also a privilege to raise your own children and to have a family."

"We'll thank you, Gary. It's also a privilege to be your friend. We have been through a lot with operation Darkfall and you pulled us through brilliantly."

"Well thank you, Jake. It's been an honor."

"But right now we have bigger fish to fry. If this goes south are you going home to your family?" Jake asked.

"Sure am, if I can. So I think I may make arrangements to be home before the big bang occurs–just in case."

"Good idea. If I were in your shoes, I would probably do the same thing–family is sacred.

They turned to Slade. He thought a minute and then said, "When the time nears I will tell my two daughters, Marla and Darla to pack a couple of suitcases each and we're going on vacation."

Slade next turned to Gary while running a hand through his thick coal black hair and ask if he had any place to go in Israel?"

"Yes we have a facility similar to yours, but not as big.

Okay, Jake stepped in, and with all seriousness in his deep voice said, "we need to get back to the original subject. Well it looks like we are all going to the White House and undoubtedly meet the President and perhaps other VIPS."

Jake and Slade turned to Gary and wanted to know what he would say. After all, he was a nuclear scientist and had many letters behind his name.

"They're going to grill us, interrogate us and shake us down to see if any loose coins fall to the floor. For all the power they have, they're scared."

"I don't blame um. This is the biggest decision in their lives. If they make it, it will lead to a different global outcome and attitude, and a different world. One much more favorable than the one we have right now. If we fail, Cheyenne Mountain here we come." Jake said while ringing his hands.

EIGHTY-TWO

Batter Up

"**O**kay, getting back to what's going on. It's hard for me to fathom what your last administration did to you. I mean, they screwed up everything, including leaving your country on the brink of World War III. They even rushed into the vaults, so to speak, and collected as much money as they could for their various bogus causes. Even the unelected bureaucrats were doing the same. I mean, I could write at least three books on all of the corruption and it wouldn't even make a scratch on an iceberg. This doesn't even compare to robbing Fort Knox because there isn't much gold left anyway. Even if there were, it wouldn't be enough. They would merely fire up the printing presses and C notes would be coming out like there was no tomorrow. And to top it off, they did this and more right before Trump took office."

"How do you know all of this, you're not even an American citizen, Gary." Jake said.

"Come on guys the whole world knows about some of this. 'Some being the key word.' "Sure, it was mostly hidden from prying eyes like some of the dealings the former President's son had his hands into because of his Father's influence. I'll let you in on a little secret. You know I have mentioned Frank Mulligan's name a few times. Well, Frank and I go back a long ways and did a lot of collaboration together in explaining the shortfalls that were included in, Path To Peril."

"How so, Slade asked in surprise."

" Years ago before I got heavily invested in science I met Frank at a couple of bank symposiums. He was a little older than me, but he was really bright and probably knew the banking industry better than anyone."

Jake chimed in, "Why would you go to a few of the bank meetings/" He asked just as surprised as his buddy, Slade. "Well I wanted to know how money works so I wouldn't be just another dumb scientist walking around wondering about it." Smart move the soldiers agreed.

"Well really it was my father that had the foresight in getting me interested in another discipline. He knew I needed a more well-rounded education than science. I took other courses like history, which by the way are very important. Also took geography so I would know my way around the planet."

"Your dad seemed very wise." Slade remarked

"He was. Well, after two days of dullness, in one of the symposiums, Frank and I decided to skip out the third afternoon before closing remarks and we headed to a good bar that Frank knew. We weren't there for the booze but for their Southern Deep Fried Chicken, with tater tots dripped in a special sauce and coleslaw that was better than that famous chicken place. We found a corner booth back in the building so we could talk freely and freely we did. We ate and drank and ate some more until they kicked us out at 3am. Frank had rheumatoid arthritis pretty bad and sometimes he had to get up and shake off the pain to be more clearer in his thoughts. The man could think out of the box better than anyone I ever knew. I wouldn't doubt if he was younger he would be working for DOGE. And, now the Left are still blaming the new administration because DOGE is trying to audit the books. After all, with all your kickbacks from your pet projects and ludicrous earmarks, your citizens' tax money is rushing down the drain with a giant swoosh sound while Congress and entrenched bureaucrats are continuing to become millionaires. Do you know your Congress has a cave full of federal benefit/retirement documents and other records for federal employees? It's called Iron Mountain! And get this—it's been going on for decades, and was started in 1955. And most of the documents are hand written. They started this before computers were viable. Sure, there are now some computers, but it's still mainly typed paper. Incidentally, as a side note, your Congress pulled out of your Social Security system at about the same time, and started their own retirement and medical systems. After all why should the people you put in office to represent you stoop so low as to have the same system as you." Gary paused for a moment to get his breath and thought what he was going to say next. "God, isn't there any honesty anywhere anymore! I'm usually not this political, but I agree with everything, Frank Mulligan said in Path To Peril. When I first read the book I was shocked at what was going on in your country, and I'm even more so today. It turns out the only thing that Congress wants to do is fight for power, line their pockets with gold and as I said earlier, be damned for the people they are supposed to serve.

Almost all of your institutions have gone totally rogue. If you don't get this straightened out and be transparent about everything, there will be a civil war and your democracy will go up in flames."

"Good God, Gary, you are scaring us again."

"You need to be scared, everyone needs to be scared. Your country needs to vote intelligently and quit voting these dumb asses into office at all levels of government. Like Thomas Jefferson said, the electorate needs to be well-informed and then vote accordingly. Today, because of your media, most of which are as corrupt as your institutions, throw out more gaslight than the cows flatulate. The simple truth is the Dems have moved away from the working men and women decades ago and now have become globalist and wealthy coastal elites. Do you know that fourteen states do not require any id when voting?"

"Really," Jake said. "That means there's no registration to vote either. Just show up or mail in your voter's ballot with any name you like. This is a great way to get more terrorists and criminal illegal immigrants to vote."

"I'm not going into all the numbers that categorically break down the classes, but for an example, there are at least 425,000 convicted felons who are illegal immigrants roaming free in your country, and I'm sure that many of them are ready to strike. The officials in Chicago has ordered to take down all of the shot spotters."

"Why would they do that?" Slade questioned, shaking his head.

"I don't rightly know, except to say that there are so many gun battles going on in the streets of Chicago that it's probably overwhelming their system. You know that Chicago is a sanctuary city right? They absolutely will not allow ICE to arrest and deport their mostly immigrant criminal population. They would rather allow them to roam the streets terrorizing and committing crimes against your citizens. Did you also know that the last White House administration enriched Iran's coffers by over 400 million and gave back over 100 billion dollars in assets. That's why the Middle East is aflame in war. I'm not going any further, because it only gets worse, and I believe the ordinary citizen may not understand all of the long term ramifications. I will complete my thoughts with this…your Congress has gotten so filthy corrupt along with your crooked institutions and bureaucrats it portends a dark, scary and controlled future! They're looting the piggybank! And soon, you might be living in a dystopian society."

EIGHTY-THREE

The White House

Five days later, the three were sitting in the situation room of the White House after being thoroughly vetted and searched by the secret service. They were introduced to Jerome Orson, the Secretary of Defense, Alfonso Grove, the chairman of the Joint Chiefs of Staff, the Press Secretary. Carolyn Aims, the Vice President JD Vance, Elon Musk and other civil and military dignitaries. It wasn't long before President Trump entered and everyone stood to greet him. The three were personally introduced to the President, JD Vance and Elon Musk, because they were intimately familiar with operation Darkfall. After everyone sat down and pleasantries were said, the Secretary of Homeland Security, Mary Stinson, stood up and began. "Operation Darkfall is the most important mission since World War II. This will change the global position of all the countries. We will have a new world that will be led by the United States. Sure, we are leading the world now, but much of it is corrupt. The new era will be much cleaner and transparent including China.

However, if we fail, the onus will be on us and the Cheyenne Mountain Complex will be our home for who knows how long. A charred and broken world will lay at our feet."

President Trump got her attention and ask her to continue. "I know all of you have been working very hard. The task at hand isn't easy. In fact it is the most essential and difficult thing we have ever endeavored—and I can't say for how long. I have spoken to many of you, including having a good contact with the military to get a good picture, and the details are mind boggling. Quantum mechanics is way beyond my purview as it is for 99 percent of the population. However, if you break it down section by section, the logic looks sound and if everything is ready, we can have a go in two weeks. I'm also privy to the reason why Iran won't be attacked for at least three months afterward. It is to allay to Russia one of the many reason why the United States wasn't responsible for this attack. One day the world will know how brilliant this was. In the meantime I will gather more information from Dr. Zimmerman, Mr. Cannon and Mr. Swanson. Even though the date is set for two weeks, it isn't set in stone. The intelligence of the Stuxnet II virus is out of this world. The people who designed and developed this are super geniuses. In my estimation, it is people who only come along every few decades and even hundreds of years, and we are so grateful to have them.

Going back in history, it reminds me in a way, about how we beat Germany in the nick of time to develop the atomic bomb. The reason why I say this is after discussing some of the details with a few of you I now know that Russia is on our heels. However, it was essential to see where Russia was in the scheme of things before we released the virus on Iran. We have known for some time that Iran was getting their technology from Russia. So it made since to see how far Russia was along the curve of Quantum Science, in order to see which direction Darkfall was going. Now, are there any questions?"

Slade looked at the President and asked, "Sir, if we fail, is the Cheyenne Mountain Complex fully operational?"

"You're Mr. Swanson, right?" The President asked before going on.

"Yes, sir, and it's an honor to be here, and please call me Slade." He stood and saluted the President.

The President looked directly at him and said, "Okay, Slade. I read your dossier and it's quite impressive, young man."

"Thank you, sir."

The President then got back on track and replied, "Yes, everything is in order and we are already receiving non-essential personnel. I might add that all the families in this room are also welcomed to check in to Cheyenne Mountain. Again, I have checked with everyone, including the military and my orders remain to stand down until we are ready. Now if everyone is an agreement I would like to hand control back to the Secretary of Homeland Security." The room was quiet.

Mary Stinson, rose from her chair and looked around the room and saw that all attendees were quiet. She gaveled the meeting adjourned. And as everyone was filing out the Vice President motioned for Jake, Slade and Gary to meet with him and the President for a few minutes. They needed more clarification before launching Darkfall.

EIGHTY-FOUR

The Oval Office

As the three entered the President's chambers in the oval office all three were duly impressed. And, they were not only impressed with the office itself, but with all the chatter and fast movement in the hallways. People were ducking in out of offices, small meetings occurring in some of the alcoves, and generally a beehive of activity.

"Mr. President, is it always this busy?" Jake inquired with a surprised look on his handsome face.

"Oh no, this is barely normal what we call a slow day, you know uneventful." President Trump said with a broad smile breaking out on his face. "I take it by all of your amazed looks on your faces; this is your first visit"

"Yes sir, Mr. President, they all said at once."

"You all may have a seat now. JD and I want to get a closer look on what's going on and to be able to recognize trouble in advance so we can take proactive action if needed. Gary would you like to go first?" The President replied looking directly at the little man. "Oh where are my manners. I want to thank you for all the hard work you have been doing on behalf of Israel."

"That's what friends are for, Gary. May I call you, Gary?"

"That's fine, sir,." He said in a humble voice.

"If I remember correctly, your country's intelligence agency, Mossad, was directly responsible in greatly slowing up Iran's nuclear ambitions with the first virus called Stuxnet I. It really knock out their centrifuges. And now, our country along with yours, has developed a far more advanced virus, using quantum mechanics and computing with the help of AI and Nano Technology called, Stuxnet II. And this will neutralize Russia's nuclear capabilities?" Before Gary could say anything, the President stood from the couch he was sitting on and moved over to where Gary was sitting. He got down on one knee and asked Gary face-to-face is this really going to work?"

Gary looked at the President in the eye and unequivocally said yes. "We have developed and tested it at least a thousand times and to be sure we went to Moscow State University (MSU) and tested it in their quantum lab." Gary now looked at Jake and Slade for their approval, turned back to the President and said it's a done deal."

JD stood up, looked at the President and interjected by saying, "I guess Jake and Slade where there to protect you? Is that right?"

"They did a lot more than protection. They were instrumental in disarming Russia's last two analog missile silos. They needed to be taken care of manually, because the virus doesn't interact with analog technology. And, I might add that it wasn't easy, especially getting at and disarming the silo at Severodvinsk."

"The reason for all these additional questions is Israel and us have spent a lot of time, effort and money on this operation and we want to make sure it's perfect, or we'll all be heading to the Cheyenne Mountain Complex." JD said amplifying the seriousness and tone of his statement.

"I have a question sir, has there been any chatter from the Russian Police Agencies and especially FSB?" Jake stated, rubbing a hand through is burnished blond hair.

"Why do you asked," the President replied.

"Well, sir, we had a couple of close calls"

"Yes I know about them, but you got away clean. If there was any smoke from this the Russian Ambassador, Mark Koslov would've been parked outside of Jerome Orson's office. If there is anything, I'm sure they would have been looking at a dead end. No, they're chasing their tails and will have nothing but a bunch of them going up dead end alleys. Now if there isn't anything else, let's get rolling–I have a lot on my plate. After their good byes. The three of them drove back to Alexandria together.

"Well can you believe that," Jake quipped. "As busy as the President is he made time out of his day to speak with us individually, and JD was there, too. What a pair of great guys!"

"Don't be too admiring," Gary said. "They were also there to learn if there were any snafus, and it looks like we miffed the Russians. Otherwise, we might have been choosing our brass plates for the right gulag. I know Gitmo has been recently opened and it's not a pleasant place, but I think it doesn't compare to one of the gulags in Siberia."

"Nothing compares to anything when you're in Siberia," the soldiers chuckled.

EIGHTY-FIVE

Day of Tragedy

It was 0500 and once again, Jake, Slade, and Gary were in the situation room. This was the day when all hell would break loose in Russia. Everything was set to go at 0800, just as everyone was sitting down and having breakfast at the Kremlin.

It was now 0700 and as they were looking at the big electronic screens on the wall, Jake noticed there wasn't too much activity going on with the Navy. As a matter of fact there wasn't much at all. It was as if everything was operating on a normal day for the Navy. He would have thought there would have been more activity on the high seas, such as a flat top or two, maybe a destroyer and some cutters to help save some of the Russian officers and seamen. If he wanted activity he only needed to look around and see all the men and women working very quietly and diligently doing their assigned tasks.

At 0800 sharp Gary would VPN to his network and remotely launch the first phase of Darkfall. The wolves, pent up for months were now ready to go and unleash their terror on the Russian Navy. Gary typed the GO words on his heavily guarded and classified network. The wolves awoke, immediately split up and smashed through the first set of gateways at the originating two sites and infiltrated their c-lines. As the beasts slashed through their servers, routers, bridges and digital CPUs they learned as they went. Just like an orchestra, the instruments where chose to perform at specific times, duration and tone to play the notes of destruction. The night runs were now continuing to smash through the gateways, servers, routers bridges and digital CPUs of each nuclear submarine. The creatures were looking for any closed distributed systems where groups of subs could communicate together within a closed system with no outside interference. Also, these brutes were looking for dark nets anywhere in their system. Moreover, they were looking for information the Russian Navy had in their iClouds. Each of the Russian nuclear submarine's reactors were now reduced to half power. This is in turn interfered with the drives of each nuclear sub and eventually reduced their speed to just one half of full ahead. Further, they learned in horror that all nuclear missiles, warheads, torpedoes and marine bombs and mines were all neutralized. By now all systems were controlled and in a Gordian Knot. It was if they were operating submarines back in the 50's. Surely this couldn't be a time warp many of the captains were thinking. They weren't in any immediate danger and they certainly could communicate to their commanders. However, the Stuxnet II virus now had control of the entire Russian Navy fleet, including the Borie-Class, Akula and Yasen-Class nuclear submarines–the pride of the Russian Navy. Everyone kept looking for an enemy but couldn't see any, because the enemy was within. What in tarnation was going on.

EIGHTY-SIX

What Happened?

The commander at Sevastopol after communicating with the other two point commanders couldn't wait any longer. He broke protocol and went straight to Admiral Aleksandr Moiseyev, the top brass of the Russian Navy. After hearing the shocking news, he didn't wait and called Vladimir Putin, the President of Russia. Without conferring with anyone, Putin put all military forces on high alert, even the reserves. He couldn't see the enemy, but suspected the United States. *I mean who else would have this kind of technology,* he thought.

After speaking with President Trump, he hung up but still kept his forces on high alert. It was now 1030 hours and still no definite news. He was fit to be tied. And now he just learned that all of the land nuclear missile sites were dead including the ICBMs and Hypersonic missiles. He now expelled the US Ambassadors from Russia and retrieved his Russian Ambassadors home from the United States. They were at a standoff, but through his ambassadors and other high level sources he realized that the United States wasn't having the same difficulty. Now he also learned that some of his nuclear submarines were having trouble keeping positive buoyancy and running at half drive. Trouble was happening so fast, he didn't have time to dither. He wasn't about to start World War III yet. For Christ sakes his country wasn't prepared. They were really caught flat footed this time. He ordered his top science officers to pool thousands of software engineers and programmers to check their systems' code to sniff out any abnormalities that would give them some idea of what was going on. *So far nothing!* He thought.

He remembered the K-141 Kursk in the Barents Sea on August 12, 2000. Russia was deeply criticized for its slow and ineffective response to save the 118 seamen on the Oscar-II class submarine. The United States offered help but was refused. Most people think Vladimir Putin is a very evil man and rightly so, but at times, he seems to have a kind heart on some things. And President Trump seems to be the only man from the West who can effectively communicate with him.

President Putin was at wits end and wasn't going to wait any longer and wanted to talk to President Trump man-to-man about this issue. He called again on the direct encrypted line.

"Yes Premier Putin, how can I help you."

" Mr. President I'm going to get to the point quickly, we have four of our subs in trouble and we don't want the Kursk tragedy replayed again. Can you help us retrieve our distressed submarines and possibly get our seamen out of trouble?"

President Trump thought for a moment and replied, "of course we can Vladimir. Basically where are they at?"

"You should know that!" The Premier exclaimed.

"Yes, that true but we don't know which ones are in trouble. Only you do." The President replied.

"There was a long pause on the call and finally, there is one in the Black Sea, one in the Barents sea, and two in the Atlantic by the Canary Islands. Do you have the equipment to get the men out safely?"

"Don't worry we'll take care of it. Just forward the correct coordinates and information to your Ambassador, Mark Koslov, and have him give the latest information to Jerome Orson, the Secretary of Defense (DOD)."

"I can't do that Mr. President."

"Why is that so?'

"Well, you probably know already that we expelled your Ambassador, Pete Knowles, from Russia and recalled our Ambassador, Mark Koslov, home to Russia."

"Why would you do that? Is there something else going on that we are not aware of?" President Trump asked with all sincerity.

Premier Putin thought about what he would say next. He needed to buy himself more time to see if his engineers could figure out what was going on. "No, everything seems fine, but for some reason, four of our subs are experiencing trouble and the on-board crew can't figure it out."

"We will help you figure it out. Are any of the crews in immediate danger, Vladimir?

"No, they're just at neutral buoyancy running at half speed."

"Okay, we'll send cutters to your GPS coordinates and get our men on board to help you with this emergency. Can we get them on board, Vladimir?"

"Yes, I suppose so because of the emergency." Vladimir fretted.

"Thank you, Mr. President. Don't thank me yet, Vladimir." The line went dead.

EIGHTY-SEVEN

Help Is On The Way

The President was in the oval office and called in his chief of staff, Robert Dye. "Hey Bob, just got a call from Vladimir Putin. It appears that four of their nuclear submarines are in trouble, and I promised him that the United States would help to retrieve the Russian officers and seamen."

"Did he say what was wrong?" Bob asked.

"No not really."

"What about the subs sir?"

"You mean are we going to confiscate them? That wasn't discussed. I think Vladimir is still worried about what happened to the Kursk, and he certainly doesn't want this to happen again. In the end we did try to help but by then they were too deep and it was too late. We did get some good photos of the 141-Kursk, Oscar class II and they were way behind us in submarine technology. Though in defense, it was an older class. Bob keep me in the loop. I want to know every detail you hear about. Also, I want Jake Cannon, Slade Swanson and Dr. Gary Zimmerman back here pronto."

"You got it sir." Bob turned on his heels and was out of the oval in a blink.

The President went to the fridge, grabbed himself a Cola, sat back in his cushy executive chair and thought how all of this was going down. *There were still a lot of details to work out*, he thought. The actual transfer of personnel wasn't his main worry, but what was Vladimir going to do. He clearly lied to him about his main problem and he wasn't sure on what the Premier was thinking. He sure as hell didn't want World War III to break out. There were to many variables that could go wrong, and go wrong quickly.

EIGHTY-EIGHT

The Transfer

"Oh fellas, I'm sure glad that you could get here so fast," Bob said to Jake, Slade and Gary. I have some good news, the two subs stuck in the Atlantic by the Canary Islands are now able to steam under their own power. But we still have the other two. One is in the Black Sea and the other in the Barents Sea. That's why you are here. Also, I'm waiting for a Russian political analyst to arrive shortly. He was at sea off the coast of Florida fishing for the big boys when he got the call. His name is Dr. Ivan Stepanov and he knows Russia and is intimately familiar with the Russian Navy. He took asylum in the United States when his marriage failed back in Russia. He has a son in the Russian Navy that's equivalent to an XO in our Navy. He hasn't seen his son in fifteen years and has only spoken to him once during that time. He is all US patriot and well trusted. He's our guy."

"Bob, Dr. Ivan Stepanov is here in the outer office."

"Well, show him in, Sam."

A large framed, bearded gentleman, with salt and pepper hair came into the office and headed straight to the President and shook his hand. "It's an honor and a privilege to meet you, sir. I believe I have spoken to you once before."

"Why yes, doctor, I remember. How was your luck with the big boys?"

"No luck other than getting a little sunburned."

After introductions were made, everyone sat on couches and the business at hand got under way. "Okay, I called you guys here to let you know how the four of you will be going into the subs interior after our seamen make the personnel transfer of their seamen through our collars. Slade, you and Dr. Zimmerman will meet Captain Mikhail Menkov. The captain is in command of a Delta Class nuclear ballistic missile submarine in the Barents Sea. You will serve as ambassadors of the United States being very diplomatic in you speech and actions. Sorry, Slade, you will not be armed except for your God given skills."

"Sir, surely their captain and senior first officer will be armed." Slade responded with concern and fear written across his face.

"This is probably true," the President said with deep reflection. "But remember you and Dr. Zimmerman are there peacefully representing the United States. I can't believe that they would kill you guys in cold blood. You will be representing me personally and you will have appropriate gifts from me to present to them—no you will be okay. Now Dr. Stepanov, you will be with Mr. Jake Cannon to serve as ambassadors just like Slade and Dr. Zimmerman. Your assignment will be to meet Captain Maxim Nevolin, commander of the Akula Class attack nuclear submarine in the Black Sea. Will fly both teams out on black hawks with extra fuel to their respective locations during the extraction of the Russian seamen. You will be lowered by a Bosun's chair and either land on top of or alongside the subs.

"Whose going to rescue us if we miss our target?" Dr. Stepanov asked with alarm in his voice. "You know I'm not in the best of shape." Mr. President. "Ivan, you'll be fine."

"Our cutters will be there before our men are lowered in Bosun's chair and will guide and collect all Russian seamen and officers and transfer them aboard the U.S. cutters and get them dry clothes and a good meal before they make a decision on where they want to go. If they apply for Asylum they undoubtedly will be granted temporary status until a more permanent solution can be arranged. The rest will be free to go back home." Mr. President replied with a little sarcasm in his voice.

EIGHTY-NINE

Dark Skies Over Russia

Vladimir Putin began to pace again. The extraction of his crew from both subs went smoothly. Some of the men decided to seek asylum and move to the U.S. while other seamen and most of the officers decided to come back home. He thought, *this was the easy part.* But he was still suspicious of the United States intentions. However, all of his brightest stars including the foremost scientist in Russia, Dr. Maxim Lenin, didn't have a clue as to what happened. Tens of millions lines of code were check time and time again and not one word or sequence was out of order, and nothing missing. It was as if a ghost changed their coded systems and left without a trace. Vladimir thought *at least they could have said thank you—leave them something!* The brightest conjectured that it must have been some sort of AI, Nano and Quantum technology possibly working together to pull off such a feat. But who in the world could produce such code and technology.

He made good on his promise and fired the director and assistant director, Dr. Boris Andreev. He kept coming back to the so called tourists that the FSB was trying to arrest. He was sure that they had something to do with the events that stopped Russia cold in its tracks. Even as crazy as people said he was, he couldn't just start firing off nukes. Wait a minute, he didn't have any nukes. Sure, he had all the equipment and machinery, but they just wouldn't fire. In all his years, even during the time he was a colonel in the KGB and saw the Berlin Wall come down. He's never seen anything like this. What happened a few days ago was at least 10 fold stranger. He thought of Dr. Strangelove where U.S. Air Force Major T.J. King Kong straddled a nuke and rode it all the way to Perdition. This was almost as crazy! He now had to prepare and meet President Trump at the Kremlin in a few days. *What was he going to say, he didn't have the foggiest!* He thought.

EPILOGUE

President Trump met Premier Vladimir Putin at the Kremlin three days later to speak with him personally, face-to-face about the incident that neutralized Russia's nuclear capabilities. He wasted no time in trying to convince Putin to understand the United States had nothing to do with the calamity. And they were just as surprised as he was. The President was all too happy to rescue some of their naval seamen and officers. He was greatly relieved that Putin didn't jump the gun and start World War III. Although, with what? It was the biggest gamble the US had ever taken. A few days later, Vladimir called the President and told him that he would probably keep his military on high alert and continue to keep his Ambassador at home. He had feelers all over the world and wanted to see if anything shook out He told President Trump that things would remain this way for a time to see if there was any evidence of the United States involvement.

However Russia and Ukraine now could make decent headway because of a lack of nuclear weapons on the Russian side. President Trump was planning on inviting the two leaders of Russia and Ukraine to the White House to suggest and guide them to make the right choices for their country and countrymen.

Moreover in the back of his mind, President Trump could see overtones of Russia looking at China. He was concerned that a war could possibly break out between Russia and China before he solidified the deal with Russia and Ukraine. *But wait a minute,* he thought. Russia doesn't have any active nukes so that wouldn't be a fair fight between the super powers. *But wait again,* he thought. Russia isn't a super power anymore. In fact it will take decades for Russia to catch up if they ever will. In the meantime the United States only has one mortal enemy to deal with.

And, after the negotiations with Ukraine and Russia he will start negotiations with President XI Jinpinp of China the following month.

And it most likely will include the arduous task of reducing missiles one at a time. President Trump hopes by doing this, other nations will follow suit. Of course, trusting the Chinese has always been a tall order for our country. But with Russia on the sidelines, the US can really concentrate and keep track of what China is doing without looking over its shoulder.

Israel and the Arab states are so delighted with what has happened that they gave most of the work to the United States to rebuild the Gaza Strip. Mossad waited six months, as planned, before pulling the plug on Iran's nuclear ambitions. Besides with the new Gaza Strip progressing, Iran was now nothing more than a ghost of what it used to be. No more

Humus, Hezbollah, Houthis, ISIS, al-Qaida, or any other terrorist's ideology. They all went back to whence they came - the sand! As far as Iran's aspirations of developing a nuclear bomb - those days were over. The global economy will no doubt improve and the golden age will be upon us with the rebuilding of Ukraine and Russia. Commerce is now the king! North Korea has lost most of its friends and has no place to go but up. But one never knows about this dark and mysterious country, and one never knows who will rear its ugly head next and challenge the United States.